"You Feel It, Too?"

His question was rough and raw, full of a husky wonder. Desire flared in his eyes. When he slanted his head, fitting his mouth at first gently then more demandingly to hers, a traitorous heat flooded her body, rendering her weak but yearning for more. The animal excitement in his kiss grew as he deepened it, parting her lips to explore the honeyed cavern of her mouth.

When Sloan pulled slightly away, Kendall trembled, her thoughts jumbled. She stood on tiptoes and brushed her lips across his, saying, "You know you didn't really have to ask that."

MARGARET RIPY

loves to travel and only writes about places she has visited. In her books there is a "little bit of herself and her experiences." Without the support and love of Mike, her husband of fourteen years, she says her writing wouldn't be possible. He has the characteristics she wants in a male hero.

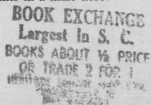

Dear Reader:

Romance readers have been enthusiastic about Silhouette Special Editions for years. And that's not by accident: Special Editions were the first of their kind and continue to feature realistic stories with heightened romantic tension.

The longer stories, sophisticated style, greater sensual detail and variety that made Special Editions popular are the same elements that will make you want to read book after book.

We hope that you enjoy this Special Edition today, and will enjoy many more.

The Editors at Silhouette Books

MARGARET RIPY
Feathers in the Wind

Silhouette Special Edition

Published by Silhouette Books New York

America's Publisher of Contemporary Romance

To my brothers,
Howard and Paul

SILHOUETTE BOOKS, a Division of Simon & Schuster, Inc.
1230 Avenue of the Americas, New York, N.Y. 10020

Copyright © 1984 by Margaret Ripy
Cover artwork copyright © 1984 Howard Rogers Inc.

Distributed by Pocket Books

ISBN: 0-671-53689-3

First Silhouette Books printing September, 1984

10 9 8 7 6 5 4 3 2 1

All of the characters in this book are fictitious. Any resem-
blance to actual persons, living or dead, is purely coincidental

Map by Ray Lundgren

SILHOUETTE, SILHOUTTE SPECIAL EDITION and
colophon are registered trademarks of Simon & Schuster, Inc.

America's Publisher of Contemporary Romance

Printed in the U.S.A.

Books by Margaret Ripy

Silhouette Romance

A Second Chance at Love #71
A Treasure of Love #170

Silhouette Special Edition

The Flaming Tree #28
Tomorrow's Memory #76
Rainy Day Dreams #114
A Matter of Pride #134
Firebird #164
Feathers in the Wind #189

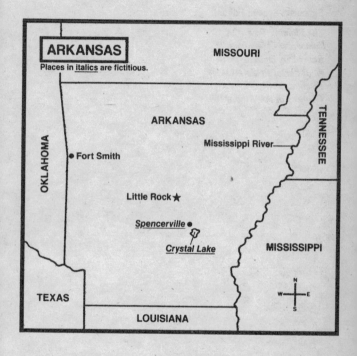

ARKANSAS

Places in _italics_ are fictitious.

MISSOURI

ARKANSAS

OKLAHOMA

● Fort Smith

Mississippi River

TENNESSEE

Little Rock ★

Spencerville ●

Crystal Lake

MISSISSIPPI

TEXAS

LOUISIANA

N
W—E
S

Chapter One

*W*ith a flip of his wrist, Sloan tossed the banana-colored Frisbee through the air, following its flight with night-dark eyes.

"I've got it!" a young girl shouted as she jumped up quickly, catching the plastic disk. With the agility of the young, Missi landed on one foot, balanced herself and immediately threw the Frisbee back toward her father.

The jarring ring of a phone cut into the quiet stillness of the hot June afternoon, turning Sloan's attention away from the Frisbee and toward the cabin. On the second ring the Frisbee was completely forgotten as Sloan started jogging toward the cabin.

"Must be your mother. Be back in a minute, hon," he tossed over his shoulder as he ran up the wooden steps to the front porch.

Inside the two bedroom cabin on Crystal Lake, he

headed for the kitchen, picking up the phone on the sixth ring. His breathing was controlled, but his muscles were automatically tensing at the prospect of talking to Sandra.

"Hunter speaking."

"Sloan, this is Sandra."

Even though he had expected his ex-wife's call, every time he talked to her, bitter and painful memories of their last few years as husband and wife would assail him. His taut, large frame conveyed he was instantly ready for anything.

"Yes?" Whenever Missi stayed with him, Sandra called almost every day. Sandra smothered their daughter, and on more than one occasion he had told her that. But she had never listened to him.

"How's Missi adjusting to this vacation you planned?"

Sloan's jaw knotted stubbornly at the tone of disdain in Sandra's voice; his grip on the phone tightened. "She's fine. Why wouldn't she be?" Wariness changed Sloan's expression as he combed his fingers through his blond hair repeatedly, a gesture of his that indicated mounting anger or frustration.

"She's had so many changes in the last eighteen months that I still don't think staying at that . . . *cabin* for six weeks was a good idea."

"Then you should have thought of that eighteen months ago. Besides, it will give you a good opportunity to get to know your new husband." Bitterness crept into his voice, a frown slashing across his tanned features.

Easy, Sloan. It had been over between them a long time ago, but the killing blow had been when Sandra had left him for another man, her new husband.

"But Crystal Lake is in the middle of nowhere. Arkansas is in the middle of nowhere!"

"I'd hardly think the people of Arkansas would say that," Sloan countered sarcastically.

"Is Missi there?" Exasperation was clearly evident in Sandra's voice.

"No, she's outside. I'll go get her." His voice was controlled again, his expression unreadable.

"No, just tell her that I'll call later on tonight. I'm already late to meet Ted for dinner." There was a pause, then the inevitable question: "Has Missi had an asthma attack?"

"No. Don't worry, Sandra. I wasn't gone so often that I don't know what to do if she does. I'll tell her you'll call later. Good-bye."

After hanging up, Sloan half sat, half leaned against the kitchen table, his thoughts churning, racing back over the past two years. His only salvation had been his research project at the university. And, according to Sandra, that was what had driven them apart and her into the arms of another man.

A scream ripped through the silence. For a timeless second, Sloan froze. Another piercing cry galvanized him into action, and he flew across the living room and out the screened door.

His black gaze darted frantically around the yard, searching for Missi, as he rushed down the steps and out into the yard. When he found her near the edge of the trees that surrounded the cabin, a paralyzing fear gripped him in a sheath of ice, and a momentary sense of panic shot up his spine. A large, mangy dog had her pinned on the ground, its low growls permeating the hot air with their deadly menace.

Sloan bent and picked up several large pebbles, then flung them at the dog. "Get out of here! Scram!"

The dog looked up in his direction, baring its teeth. Sloan threw another rock at the mongrel, missing it by a few inches, but the mutt backed away from Missi, its growls sounding more lethal. Again, Sloan aimed one rock, then another, at the dog, each hitting its target and finally sending the dog scurrying into the woods.

Missi lay huddled on the ground in a ball, whimpering, her breathing rapidly becoming labored. Sloan was at her side in an instant, cradling his daughter to him, whispering soothing words as he rocked her back and forth. Missi started wheezing, her breathing ragged, her face ashen.

"The dog's gone, hon. You'll be all right now. Take a deep breath. Nice and easy, hon." Concern etched deep lines of worry into Sloan's face.

He had to get her into the cabin and give Missi her medicine before the asthma attack became worse. If only he hadn't . . .

He let that thought go unfinished as he swung his daughter up into his arms, noticing for the first time the bite on her left forearm. He looked down at Missi, her face like a bleached sheet. She clung desperately to him as she cried against his shoulder, struggling to breathe, each effort a gasp.

A tightly coiled steel band constricted his own chest. His heartbeat throbbed and at that moment he could have killed. If he had been a minute later, his daughter could have been seriously injured by that stray dog.

Inside the cabin Sloan placed Missi on her bed, smoothing her hair back, telling her to relax. After handing her a glass of warm water, he gave her the asthma medicine she always had with her. As Missi's breathing became more even, Sloan held her to him and talked about anything that came to mind to make her forget about the dog attack. Her asthma had been worse this past year since the divorce and the move to Atlanta with Sandra and Ted. When she could no longer cope with a problem, Missi invariably had an asthma attack.

Finally when Missi was calm and out of danger, Sloan examined her arm. "I'm going to get an antiseptic to clean this bite. Then we'd better go into Spencerville and have a doctor look at it."

"Daddy, that dog was so big. It came running out of the woods straight at me. I . . ."

"Shh, hon. Don't think anymore about it. I'll take care of everything."

But as Sloan rose to go into the bathroom, he felt his own impotent rage at the dog and himself. *My God, my daughter could have been killed by that damned dog! Why in the hell wasn't I there when she needed me?* Sloan berated himself as he searched for the antiseptic.

Too many times in the past he hadn't been there. He

wouldn't let the attack ruin the plans that Missi and he had made for their six-week vacation. He loved his daughter and he had a lot to make up for.

Dr. Kendall Spencer sat in her office scribbling a few hurried notes on a chart while she had a couple of minutes before her last patient for the day. Pausing to take a sip of coffee, she scanned the clutter on her desk, then impatiently brushed stray strands of short black hair away from her face. She frowned, weariness canceling the usual sparkle in her gray eyes.

Why is it I never seem to find the time to catch up? she silently asked herself, a heavy sigh escaping her slightly parted lips.

With the summer months ahead, her work load would certainly increase. Over the past few years, Crystal Lake had drawn many vacationers during the summer months and at the moment she wished she had taken her grandmother's advice and gone on a vacation at the end of April. But two of her pregnant patients had been near their due date and she hadn't wanted to be away from Spencerville in case one of them had gone into labor a couple of weeks early. She knew Dr. Hatfield, in Conway, would have covered for her, but the truth was she hadn't wanted to go on a vacation alone, and her grandmother had complained she was too old to start going to the beach.

Too old? Kendall had never thought of Maria Spencer as too old to do anything. Her grandmother was always so alive and vital, but then again, recently . . .

A short rap on her office door caught Kendall's attention. "Yes, Bonnie?"

Her nurse poked her head into the office. "Flora is in room one, Kendall."

Kendall offered Bonnie a weak smile. "Good. That means I might get home on time tonight—provided there's not another emergency like yesterday."

"How's Timmy doing?"

Kendall frowned as she recalled the previous evening. Timmy's parents had brought him into the clinic as she was leaving; the six-year-old had caught his leg in the tractor on their farm.

"It's a miracle, but the surgeon who operated on Timmy in Little Rock was able to save his leg. He won't run for a while, but at least he'll be all right in a few months." Kendall stood, stretched her cramped muscles, then started for the door.

"Did you get any sleep last night?" Bonnie stepped aside to allow Kendall to precede her out into the hallway.

"I think about an hour early this morning. I returned from Little Rock at four, but I was so keyed up it took several hours before I fell asleep."

"Did you run into Blake at the hospital?"

Kendall stopped outside room one, her body stiff, her eyes narrowing in disapproval. "Bonnie, I know we've been friends for years, but you also know how I feel about the subject of one Dr. Blake Mathews. It's a closed one and certainly not one to be mentioned at work." Kendall's tone was businesslike, but her stern look softened at the hurt expression on her friend's face. She smiled, placing her hand on the doorknob. "I'm sorry, Bonnie. I didn't mean to come down on you so hard. It's been a long day. But to answer your question, yes. In fact, Blake was the surgeon who operated on Timmy. The reunion was less than pleasant."

Opening the door to room one, Kendall became the complete doctor as she politely greeted Flora Baker, a sixty-year-old patient who had a high-blood-pressure problem.

After she examined Flora, Kendall wrote out a refill prescription for Flora's blood-pressure medicine. "I don't know why I'm bothering, Flora Baker. I strongly suspect you have at least one full bottle at home."

The older woman's gaze lowered to the floor. "I keep forgetting. I've never liked taking pills, Kendall."

Even though Kendall's grandmother was twenty years older than Flora, the two ladies were good friends and Kendall had always thought of Flora as an aunt. "I'm not going to lecture you. Besides, I know it won't do any good." She took Flora's wrinkled hands in hers and looked her directly in the eye. "But it's important to take your medicine if you're going to control your blood pressure. What would this town do if anything happened to you? Who would organize the Fourth of July Arts and Crafts Fair? You know that's a main event around here."

A twinkle sparkled in Flora's brown eyes. "Kendall Spencer, I've known you since the day you were born. I know you've been the full-time doctor for this town for the past two years, but it's still hard for me not to think of you in pigtails climbing my cherry tree and eating so many cherries that you would get sick.''

"Half the people over fifty tease me about one thing or another. I don't know if I'll ever live down some of my antics as a child." A bright light gleamed in Kendall's eyes, making them appear almost silver. "It was hard enough convincing some of the people here to trust a woman to be their doctor."

The expression on Flora's lined face became serious. "We're glad, though, that you decided to go in with your father. A Spencer has taken care of this town since the day it was founded. You're one of us. And it didn't take all that long to convince those few people who thought the only place a woman should be is in the kitchen, especially when one was in a great deal of pain." Flora laughed softly. "Gus Mallard didn't have a chance."

Gus had been the last holdout, a burly old man of seventy who had been accidentally shot while hunting with his best friend. "It's hard to refuse help when your back side is full of buckshot."

Kendall turned to put away some instruments. Small towns didn't always open their arms wide to a stranger, especially a doctor who would be responsible for their well-being. Spencerville was no different. The folks she had known and loved all her life had been visibly relieved when four years before she had returned to assist her father, who had been the only doctor for miles around. Not two years later her father had died from a stroke, leaving her as the sole doctor to care for the people of Spencerville and the surrounding countryside.

She was actively looking for a doctor to share the practice with her, but it wouldn't be easy to find one. At one time she had thought Blake might be that doctor. But she had discovered the hard way that a woman didn't always know a man, even though she had dated him for over a year.

"Kendall, I'll promise to try this time, but it ain't gonna be easy to remember. I only have a few more weeks to get everything in order for the fair."

Flora and Kendall left the examination room and made their way toward the clinic's reception area.

"Why don't you put them next to your toothbrush, so when you brush your teeth, you'll remember?"

Flora tilted her head at an angle, her smile broad. "It's not common knowledge, but I don't have a tooth in my head. I think, though, I'll put them near the glass I put my dentures in at night." At the door leading into the reception room, Flora hesitated, facing Kendall. "Maria is gonna enter her pottery this year? It's a bunch of nonsense, her thinking that winning every year doesn't encourage others to try."

"You know Grandma. She prefers to give her pieces away rather than sell them. Money and blue ribbons mean nothing to her."

"Well, then, she'll at least display some of her latest pieces, won't she?"

Laughter rolled from Kendall's throat, the tired lines in her face wiped away. "No. She figures everyone in town has at least one piece of her pottery, so why see anymore."

"But not just the townspeople come to the fair," Flora protested in an exasperated voice.

"Tell that to Grandma. You know how stubborn she can be when she sets her mind on something."

The outer door to the clinic opened, and Kendall's attention strayed from Flora to the man and young girl who entered. The first thing that hit Kendall as her gaze rested upon the man was the darkness of his eyes, almost black, which was in complete contrast to the blondness of his hair. That observation, though, was quickly replaced by a sense of iron discipline and an element of sensual danger that surrounded the man. It was evident in his roughly chiseled features, the way he moved toward Bonnie with a natural self-confidence that heightened Kendall's feminine awareness of him. She strongly sensed that when he entered a room, heads turned in his direction.

Kendall mentally shook herself, appalled at her intense reaction to a total stranger. She must be more exhausted than she thought!

She tore her gaze away from him and toward the young girl next to him. The child's eyes were red from crying. Quickly Kendall's regard traveled over the slim girl, trying to assess what was wrong, at the same time advancing into the reception room.

"My daughter has been bitten by a dog," the man was explaining to Bonnie.

For a few seconds the stranger's deep, husky voice, seductively low, sent alarm signals through Kendall, but hastily she dismissed them. The little girl needed medical attention! She was holding her arm, her small hand covering a bandaged area.

"Bring her this way and let me take a look at her arm," Kendall said to the stranger's back.

He spun around and pinned her with an appraising look, quickly shifting his incredibly dark eyes to take in her whole length. Kendall's consciousness became centered in sensations, the warmth his absorbing regard was creating in her, the musky tang of him that was drifting to her, the deep, liquid look entering his eyes as they stared into hers.

"You are the doctor?" Disbelief sounded in his voice.

"Yes," Kendall replied calmly, even though she was momentarily disconcerted by the bold recklessness of his survey. "The only one," she couldn't help but add.

The woman before him was too young to be a doctor. This was Sloan's first thought as again his eyes swiftly journeyed down the length of her. And beautiful, he added silently, his gaze magnetically drawn back to her soft gray eyes, fringed in long black lashes.

Missi shifted beside him, and Sloan reluctantly pulled his attention away from the woman in front of him. He placed a hand on his daughter's shoulder and said, "Missi was bitten by a stray dog about two hours ago. I think she needs stitches."

"I'm Dr. Kendall Spencer." She extended her hand, but she wasn't quite prepared for the jolt of electricity that shot up her arm as the stranger's hand closed over hers. Her eyes widened briefly before she managed to gather her poise about her. "Come this way, Mr.—"

For some reason Sloan found himself hating to relinquish her hand, but he did. "I'm Sloan Hunter and this is my daughter, Missi."

Sloan followed Dr. Kendall Spencer through the doorway and down a long hall, still not quite able to believe she was a doctor, but most of all the intense response she had produced in him when they had shaken hands a few moments before. Her touch had seared him, a lingering warmth still in his hand even moments later.

While Sloan observed as Kendall cleansed Missi's bite, then gave his daughter six stitches, any doubts that he might have had about her being a doctor were eliminated. Dr. Kendall Spencer was professional but gentle as she handled Missi, explaining in a quiet voice to his daughter everything she was doing.

Kendall glanced up and into Sloan's midnight-dark eyes. What she was about to say completely flew from her mind as the unnerving impact of Sloan's gaze struck her with its full force. She felt trapped by the power of him, the sheer intensity of his regard creating a quickening of her heartbeat.

Sloan's mouth curved into a knowing smile, as though he, too, had sensed the invisible bond that had leaped across the room, linking them together. A burning warmth radiated from his eyes, welding them even closer together.

All Kendall could manage was a fragile smile that

barely touched the edges of her mouth as she dropped her gaze back to Missi and compelled herself to concentrate totally on the injured girl before her. But it was difficult with Sloan Hunter standing only three feet away, watching, with an unwavering directness, every move she made.

Chapter Two

$\mathscr{M}$ r. Hunter, I'd like to see you in my office for some information on Missi," Kendall said after taking care of the young girl's bite. Turning to Missi, she added, "If you'll go with Bonnie, she'll show you the waiting room that's set up especially for children."

Sloan started to say something but decided against it when he saw the concern in Kendall's eyes. There was something that she wanted to say to him without Missi's presence. Dread leadened his steps as he followed Kendall into her office.

"Have a seat, Mr. Hunter." Kendall indicated a chair, then sat down behind her desk. "Do you have the dog penned?"

"No. Why . . ." Sloan stopped. *Rabies!*

"Then you have no way of knowing if the dog that bit Missi has had its rabies shots?"

Sloan shook his head, a grim expression descending on his face.

"If you can't locate the dog soon, then Missi will have to have the rabies shots."

"No!" Sloan said instantly, thinking of all the horror stories he had heard about the shots. No, he couldn't put his child through that!

"Mr. Hunter, you don't have a choice." Kendall's voice softened. Her features gentled into a warm smile. "I know what you're thinking, but let me reassure you the series of shots used today is nothing like a few years ago."

Some of his distress eased. "How many shots does she have to have?" he asked.

"Only five over a month's time—and in the arm, not the stomach. They aren't nearly as painful and traumatic as before."

Sighing, Sloan leaned back in his chair and relaxed a little. "I realize I have no choice. Rabies is deadly and that dog could certainly have had it. But let me tell Missi. She's got asthma, and any extremely stressful situation could bring on an attack."

"Oh, I see. We can start the vaccine anytime after tomorrow. It will take a day to get the vaccine from Little Rock. I would suggest contacting the sheriff's office and having them help you look for the dog. Where was Missi when the dog bit her?"

"We're staying in a cabin by the lake for five more weeks. She was playing outside when the dog came out of the woods."

"Did she provoke the dog?"

A flicker of anger sparked Sloan's eyes. "No! Missi loves animals."

"I only asked because if the attack was unprovoked, then it's more likely to mean the dog has rabies than if she had provoked the dog."

"No," Sloan answered in a calmer voice. "When I came out of the cabin the dog had Missi pinned to the ground, ready to bite her again."

Kendall was overcome by a strong impulse to move from behind her desk and comfort Sloan Hunter. She could imagine the fear that had run through his mind when he had seen the dog towering over his child, ready to tear into her. He was a man capable of handling many emergencies coolly and calmly, she sensed, but there was a certain vulnerability where his daughter was concerned.

She stood. "I'll order the vaccine. Call me when you're ready to start the shots this week."

Sloan rose from the chair in one fluid movement, his body exuding a dazing sexuality, the muscled power of some predatory creature. Kendall found her attention centered on the man before her and for one static moment she became lost in the compelling darkness of his eyes.

You intrigue me. His onyx eyes imparted the thought across the short distance that separated them. His gaze traced the outline of her lips with a sensual leisure that constricted her throat. Then moving lower, his very male look regarded her in bold admiration. His penetrating eyes probed with flaming warmth, electrifying her senses, and she grew weak from the power of his intense appraisal.

He grinned wryly. "When I was growing up, why wasn't I lucky enough to have such a beautiful doctor to attend to my injuries?"

The rich timbre of Sloan's voice flowed over Kendall and broke the hypnotic hold he had over her. She ignored the teasing tone in his voice and walked past him toward the door. His hand reached out and ringed her wrist in a deceptively gentle manacle. His touch managed to hint at his potential strength, but at the same time was a loose bond.

The searing brand of his hand sent a strange lulling force through her and a helpless panic attacked her senses. The seductive power of his eyes left no doubt that the man only inches from her was all male. It was evident in his stance, the way he moved with an athletic prowess, his manner of self-assurance which wasn't feigned.

From years of experience, she was able to muster a cool façade and to look pointedly at his hand that held hers, then questionably at his face.

"Earlier when we came in, you were about to leave for the day, weren't you?"

His question caught her off guard and her eyes widened. "Yes." His hand lingered on her wrist and an overwhelming intoxication, produced from his touch, flooded her and was deeply disarming.

Seeing her discomfort, Sloan released her, but amusement lifted his mouth into a smile. "Good. Then I hope you'll allow Missi and me to take you to dinner. That's the least we can do after delaying you."

She placed several feet between them, his distinctive male scent wafting to her and endangering her common sense. "I'm used to delays and interruptions, Mr. Hunter. Doctors don't always have normal hours. People don't get sick or hurt between nine and five."

He laughed, deep in his throat, a sound of pure sensuality. "True, Kendall. But still I would like to take you to dinner." He also found himself wanting to pull her to him and smooth the exhaustion from her features, to kiss her lips, which had parted slightly in surprise when he had used her first name.

"Mr. Hunter, you don't . . ."

"Please. Sloan. I have a feeling we will be seeing a lot of each other over the next few weeks." His eyebrow arched upward in mockery at her startled look. "Remember, the five rabies shots?"

The ringing of the telephone on her desk afforded her a chance to regain her usual poise. She hurriedly answered it, her voice almost a whisper.

"Dr. Spencer speaking."

"Kendall, it's Blake."

Her body grew rigid, her knuckles white from her tight grip on the phone. "Yes?" she questioned warily.

Blake's laugh vibrated across the wires. "You don't sound too pleased to be hearing from me. There was a time when you were."

"Why have you called, Blake? Timmy's all right, isn't he?"

"I just thought I would give you a personal update on

our patient. In fact, Timmy is doing better than I thought. He's won the heart of every nurse on the pediatrics floor.''

"Good. Is there anything else?" Kendall fought to keep her voice level, but inside her stomach was churning. At one time she and Blake had been very serious, that was only until she had made it known she would be staying on in Spencerville to practice after her father's death and had no intention of moving to Little Rock or anywhere else. She shook, thinking of the cruel things Blake had said to her that evening. The one that hurt the most had been that she was cold and unfeeling, that any caring tenderness she had was reserved for her patients.

"I'd like to see you when you come up to look in on Timmy."

"No. You made your feelings known." Kendall glanced at Sloan, then turned her back on him and lowered her voice. "Haven't you forgotten something?"

"What?"

"Your new wife," she clipped out between clenched teeth, then carefully, with immense control, placed the receiver back in its cradle.

Drawing in a calming breath, she pasted a smile on her mouth, then twisted around, coming face to face with Sloan. "I think I'll take you up on that offer of dinner . . . Sloan."

His devilishly wayward smile chased away the coldness of Blake's voice. The scars of Blake's accusations were deep and not completely healed. For the past two years she had questioned many times if she were capable of an intimate relationship with a man. Maybe she did pour all her feelings into her patients.

"I'm glad you took pity on Missi and me."

"Pity?"

"Otherwise, Missi and I would be wandering around this town searching for the best place to eat. Now, we no longer have that worry. You can pick the place." There was laughter mixed with the words as he opened the door to her office and waited for her to pass him.

"You wouldn't have wandered too far. There are only four places to eat in Spencerville, and all of them are good."

Kendall sensed his nearness as they walked beside each other down the long hallway to the children's waiting room. The atmosphere in her office had been charged with his masculine presence. Sloan Hunter dominated a room when he was in it, and suddenly Kendall had an urge to find out more about him.

Suddenly, she came to an abrupt halt. Sloan stopped, too, a question in his eyes.

Kendall had always been straightforward, so she asked him what was on her mind. "Are you married?"

He chuckled softly. "No. Most women would have skirted that question and asked me in a roundabout way."

"But I'm not most women."

"That I'm finding out quickly." He leaned around her and opened the door to the waiting room. *And interesting*, he added to himself. Dr. Kendall Spencer had sparked his male curiosity from the beginning. A woman of contrast, he decided as he followed her into the waiting room. Very professional, but compassionate. He sensed underneath her cool exterior was a woman who was passionately alive.

"Ready to go and eat, Missi. Kendall's going to show us the best restaurant in town."

A pout tugged at Missi's mouth as she looked from her father to Kendall, then back to Sloan. "I'm not very hungry, Daddy."

"Well, then I think I'll eat your dinner. I'm starved." He placed an arm about his daughter's shoulder and grinned down at her. "Come on and keep me company while I satisfy my ravenous appetite. Who knows, you might even decide to eat something since neither one of us ate a big lunch." Sloan glanced toward Kendall, explaining, "When they handed out cooking skills, Missi and I were at the back of the line."

"I'm surprised we didn't meet. When other girls were learning to cook and sew, I was learning to bandage and nurse sick animals or anybody who would let me."

"Ah, I knew we would have something in common."

Kendall tried to ignore the growing frown on Missi's face, but it was hard to, and Kendall was having second thoughts about going to dinner with them.

She started to back out when Sloan said, "Let's get going before my stomach rebels."

What harm would one dinner do? Kendall thought, shrugging off the apprehension that had suddenly blanketed her.

Outside Kendall walked toward her car, but Sloan halted her step. "Ride with us and I'll bring you back after dinner to pick up your car. We can all squeeze into mine.''

She eyed his small sports car, the only other automobile in the parking lot except hers and Bonnie's, and shook her head. ''The place I'm taking you to would be out of your way. It's on Crystal Lake. Why don't you follow me?''

She needed time alone to compose herself. She was drawn to this man more than she wanted to admit. But the situation wouldn't be a simple one. Not only was he not from around Spencerville, but his daughter was possessive of her father's time. They were two very good reasons to stay away from Sloan Hunter.

''Okay. You lead. I'll follow.'' Humor glittered in his eyes, a rakish grin on his face.

On the fifteen-minute drive to Crystal Lake, Kendall managed to put her meeting with Sloan in perspective. He was just a man who would be here with his daughter for a few weeks this summer. That was all, she told herself until she climbed out of the car at the café and his gaze captured hers across the top of his sports car, a strong, almost tangible chain. A sensual awareness of the other surged between them and for a brief moment nothing else existed but the two of them.

''Daddy, I thought you said you were hungry,'' Missi whined. ''I'm getting hungry, too.''

Kendall blinked, the visual contact broken. That brief, searing moment made a mockery out of her earlier declaration that he was just a man who would be here with his daughter for a few weeks, then be gone, out of her life. In that instant when she had stared into his dark eyes, she had felt a strong tie with him that both excited and frightened her. She wanted to prove that Blake was wrong about her, but what if he wasn't?

Inside the café they were seated in a booth by a picture window that overlooked Crystal Lake. Missi made it a point to sit next to her father while Kendall, relieved, was left to sit across from him. But as soon as Kendall lifted her eyes and met Sloan's across the table, she realized there was no place safe from him. His blatant masculinity was as strong—perhaps even more, facing him and having to look into his eyes—as if she had been next to him.

After ordering freshwater catfish for all of them, Sloan leaned back, studying Kendall for a moment. "Is it a coincidence that your last name is Spencer and the town is called Spencerville?"

"No. My great-great-grandfather was the first doctor in this area and the people were so grateful to him that they named the town after him. Since then my great-grandfather, grandfather and father have been the town doctors."

"And you're carrying on the tradition."

"Ever since I can remember I followed my father around, learning from him. The people in Spencerville are like my family. Did you grow up in a small town or a big city?"

The smile lines at the corners of his eyes deepened. "Chicago. I've never lived in a town smaller than St. Louis, where I live now."

"And except for living in Nashville while I went to

college and medical school, this small town is the only home I've known.''

A vehement intensity shone in Kendall's eyes as she talked about the town and its people. She laughed softly as she thought of her first year away from Spencerville. Seeing the puzzled expression in Sloan's eyes, Kendall explained, ''I hated the 'big city' that first year away from here, and by the last day I tolerated the place. I don't believe I ever got used to the faster pace or the noise.''

''Oh, but look at all the things there are to do in a big city. What do you do on a Saturday night in Spencerville?''

''Go into Little Rock,'' Kendall quipped.

Before Sloan could retort, the waitress brought their dinners and placed the plates in front of them, smiling at Kendall. ''I heard the news earlier. How's Timmy doing?''

''He was lucky, Jackie. He'll be able to walk,'' Kendall answered.

''I'm having trouble again. Can I stop by the clinic tomorrow and see you before I have to be here?'' Jackie's tone lowered to a confidential level. ''Things aren't working out.''

''Sure. Just let Bonnie know when tomorrow morning.''

After Jackie left, a silence reigned at the table as everyone began eating the catfish. Kendall had been so interested in her conversation with Sloan earlier that she hadn't realized Missi hadn't said one word. In fact, a permanent frown seemed to be carved into the young girl's features, especially when she looked at Kendall.

After the edge had been taken off Sloan's appetite, he questioned Kendall further about Spencerville and Crystal Lake. They discussed the merits of various fishing spots, with Sloan declaring he was determined to learn what the leisure life was like. He pointedly tried to include Missi in the conversation, but her replies were always one-word sentences.

The atmosphere was definitely strained, Kendall thought as Jackie cleared away the dinner plates. "Did I tell you, Missi, this café is known statewide for the best piece of chocolate cake you've ever tasted?"

"No." The girl glared down at her water glass.

"I haven't had one of their pieces of cake in ages. Will you join me and have one, too?" Kendall tried again.

"No."

"But I will, Kendall. Chocolate is definitely a weakness of mine." Sloan turned to Jackie and ordered two pieces of chocolate cake.

"Then I'll have to remember that," Kendall said, trying to interject some lightness into the tension that was rapidly building at the table.

Sloan's knee brushed hers and Kendall felt as if she had been scorched. Their eyes embraced, his blazing with unabashed interest. The knowledge that he wanted her startled Kendall, but what shocked her the most was that she wanted him, too! Her fingers ached to trace the hard planes of his face, to caress the uncompromising lines of his jaw, to press her lips to his firm, sensual mouth as her hands explored his muscled leanness. For some unknown reason, she suddenly felt this man could give her life meaning and bring her a fulfillment that was lacking.

She straightened and sat back. Her exhaustion, the hostility emanating from Missi and the confusing, over-powering sensations that Sloan Hunter was causing in her were undermining her common sense, distorting things in her mind. For a moment, she actually had felt that Sloan would play an important part in her life. That thought was ridiculous, of course!

"I hate to eat and run, but my last twenty-four hours have been hectic," Kendall said after finishing her cake.

"And we need to be going, too. Missi's mother will be calling later on." Sloan laid some money on the table to cover the bill, then slid from the booth.

"Daddy, I need to go to the restroom."

"Go ahead, hon. I'll wait for you by the car."

Missi looked from Sloan to Kendall, indecision in her expression, then turned abruptly and headed for the ladies' lounge. Kendall could see the young girl hadn't wanted to leave Sloan and her alone even for a few minutes.

"I'll walk you to your car," Sloan said, his hand touching Kendall's waist to guide her.

His virile masculinity was working on her as they walked from the café and toward their parked cars. It passed through his fingers into her and it took all of Kendall's willpower not to melt into him, seeking more than his light touch on her back.

At the car Kendall turned to thank Sloan for dinner, but all words of thanks were obliterated by the devastating appeal in his eyes. She was transfixed by it, mesmerized by it.

He stepped forward, taking her head within his hands, their breath mingling. Desire flared to life in his eyes and burned into her. When he slanted his head, fitting his mouth at first gently, then more demandingly, to hers, a traitorous heat flooded her body, rendering her weak but yearning for more. The animal excitement in his kiss grew as he deepened it, parting her lips to explore the honeyed cavern of her mouth.

When Sloan pulled slightly away, his hands still framing her face, Kendall trembled, her thoughts jumbled. His hands drifted down to her shoulders, then lower, his arms loosely about her. The sensuous firelight in his dark eyes intensified as they stared at each other.

"You feel it, too?" His question was rough and raw, full of a husky wonder.

Kendall nodded, not trusting her voice to speak. This man before her in only a few short hours had become important to her. She had always been so sensible, never doing anything impulsive, that the realization made her want to turn and flee before she got in over her head.

But Kendall didn't. Instead, she stood on tiptoes and brushed her lips across his, saying, "You know, you didn't really have to ask that."

His low chuckle was laced with a warm, male arrogance that spoke of his confidence. "No, I . . ."

"Daddy, let's go. I don't want to miss Mommy's

call." Missi was standing by the front of Sloan's sports car, the pout in place.

The moment splintered into a hundred brittle fragments. Slowly the passion within Sloan's eyes was banked, and his lips quirked into an enticing smile that further disrupted Kendall's emotional equilibrium. In his eyes she saw the promise of another time when things would be settled between them, when there would be no interruptions.

"Okay, hon," he replied over his shoulder, then turned back to Kendall. "I'll call you tomorrow after I've talked with Missi about the shots," he said in a low voice.

His arms fell to his sides, leaving Kendall strangely cold, empty. Confused by her reaction to Sloan, she attempted a smile that didn't quite reach her eyes. "Fine. I'll get the vaccine."

She kept the strained half smile on her face until she had driven her car from the parking lot and was heading home. A taut ribbon of tension, from half-aroused emotions, tightened the muscles in her neck, and she kneaded the tops of her shoulders as she negotiated the highway. That look of promise in his eyes shook her. It sought to possess her, to claim what she wasn't sure she was capable of giving to another human being.

Again Kendall could hear Blake's accusation as though he were in the car with her and shouting them at her again. "Kendall, you're cold. How do you expect a man to find satisfaction if you keep him at such a distance? I've seen you more loving and caring toward those damned people in Spencerville than you are toward me."

Even though Blake was a doctor, too, he had always expected her to drop everything when he had wanted to do something or when he had come down from Little Rock to see her on those rare occasions. Never mind that she had a baby to deliver or a sick patient running a high fever. The world had always revolved around Dr. Blake Mathews, a prominent surgeon, and she wasn't allowed to have her own life if it was to interfere with his.

"That's enough, Kendall Spencer. Don't let Blake ruin things for you now after two years," she whispered to herself, but it would be hard to forget the things he had said; he had made her question her own desirability.

Sloan watched Kendall drive away, perplexed by the instant chemistry that had flared between them. Maybe he had been working too hard. He wasn't a man who rushed into anything. He always took his time, but a few minutes before he had wanted to plunge into an affair with Kendall Spencer, not even taking the time to consider the consequences, of which there were many— one being his daughter, he reminded himself. This was her six weeks.

"Daddy, let's go now."

Sloan shrugged off his bewildering thoughts and climbed in behind the wheel of his car. He drove slowly back to the cabin, dreading what he would have to say to Missi when they arrived. He understood the insecurity she was feeling. She needed to be reassured he still loved her, even though he and Sandra were divorced.

Once they were inside the cabin, Sloan came quickly to the point. "Missi, I need to talk to you."

Missi withdrew behind a defiant front. "I wanted to have dinner with just you, Daddy," she quickly said in her defense.

"That isn't what I want to talk with you about, but I do think later we need to discuss your behavior. Unless I can locate the dog that bit you, Missi, you'll have to have the rabies shots."

"Like Tiger has once a year?"

"Not quite like your friend's dog, but similar. It's to protect you from getting rabies the same way Tiger's shot is to protect him. But you'll have five of them during the next month."

"Five," Missi whispered, shifting her weight from one foot to the other, something she did when she was upset.

Sloan knelt down in front of Missi and grasped her upper arms, forcing her attention on him. "They will be no different from any other shot you've had."

"But, Daddy, I hate shots!" Her voice rose to a shrill level.

"We don't have a choice in the matter."

Sloan noticed Missi's breathing was becoming shallow, her face pinching into a tensed expression, and he hastily sought to divert her attention from the shots. "Why don't you call Mommy and see if she's home yet?"

Her breathing evened and Missi's eyes brightened at the suggestion. "Yes!"

Slowly, Sloan became relieved as Missi talked with

Sandra on the phone. Thank goodness she was back from dinner. The tension of the day began to ebb until Missi held the phone out for him to speak to Sandra.

He forced a grin to his mouth, whispering to Missi to get ready for bed. He might as well break the news to Sandra about the rabies shots, and he didn't want Missi to become upset if she overheard them arguing.

When Missi had left the kitchen, Sloan braved the consequences. "Yes?"

Sandra's voice was tight with anger when she replied. "Missi said she had to go see a doctor today because a dog bit her. What happened, Sloan?"

"What she said is true." He silently berated himself for not listening to Missi's conversation with her mother.

"She also said something about some shots."

"Yes, unless I can find the dog, she'll have to have the rabies shots."

"Oh, my God, Sloan! She has a fit every time she has to have a shot! Send her home immediately. She can have them here, where I can look after her."

Sandra didn't have to add, "Better than you," because it was apparent from her tone of voice. Anger slashed deep lines across Sloan's ruggedly hewn features. "No! It's my problem."

"But I'm her mother."

"And I'm her father. For once I think you need to realize that. I'm to have her for six weeks, and I won't let her down by sending her home. She stays."

"Sloan . . ."

"Good-bye, Sandra."

Sloan replaced the receiver in its cradle, then took the

phone off the hook. It was about time Sandra faced the fact that he was capable of raising their daughter, too. From the very first Sandra had wanted to do it all, excluding him until he had found refuge in his work.

And here he was, insanely considering an involvement with Dr. Kendall Spencer after having been burned once. He knew only too well the emotional dangers of beginning a relationship with Kendall. Their lives were separate, divided by hundreds of miles. Earlier that evening if he hadn't discovered anything else about her, he had recognized her extreme devotion to her practice and Spencerville. He had the same type of devotion and love for his work as a biochemist at the research facility at the university. Nothing could come of a relationship with Kendall, not when he had to return to St. Louis in five weeks. But that thought didn't make it any easier when Sloan went to bed that night and dreamed of Kendall Spencer.

Chapter Three

*T*he blond stranger with the midnight-dark eyes took her into his arms, gently pressing her back onto the bed. His kiss was a fiery demand that elicited a moan of pleasure from her. His hands were a tool of adoration that sought out each secret place of desire, then worked its magic. His husky growls were filled with arousal, her own fevered yearning quickly matching his.

Kendall rolled over, hugging her pillow to her as though it were the blond stranger. She reached up to run her fingers through his thick hair and instead caressed air. Her eyes snapped open. It had only been a dream. A dream that had left her very dissatisfied, she acknowledged to herself as she slowly sat up in bed and orientated herself to her bedroom, not the bedroom in the dream.

For a moment she was disappointed until she placed a

firm grip on her reeling senses, which had been ignited by the sensuous dream. Sloan Hunter had invaded her life thoroughly and totally. She couldn't even go to bed in peace without thinking about him—wanting him.

This was not sensible, she told herself as she slipped from her bed and did her usual morning stretches. How could she allow a man to have this effect on her when she had only been around him for one evening, and not even alone at that? Thoughts of Blake had never done this to her.

She had been working too hard lately, and when she saw him later on, she was sure he wouldn't have this all-engrossing effect on her. After all, she only had to keep reminding herself there could be no future in a relationship with him. Blake had lived in Little Rock, a little over an hour away, and their relationship had dissolved partially because of the distance. St. Louis was hundreds of miles away!

Kendall finished her bends, then headed for the bathroom, where she turned on the shower, letting the water rush through her fingers until it was a comfortable temperature. Quickly stripping out of her nightgown, she stepped into the stall and hurriedly showered. She had a full patient load that day, and with Jackie coming in without an appointment, it would be even busier.

Standing in front of the mirror in the bathroom, Kendall paused in putting on her makeup and touched her lips. Sloan's kiss burned in her memory, as if he had branded her his.

"Come on, Kendall," she muttered to herself. This wasn't putting him in his proper place. Quickly she put on her lipstick, as though that would eradicate the haunting impression of his kiss.

After dressing in brown slacks and a beige cotton blouse, Kendall made her way to the kitchen, where her grandmother would have breakfast ready for her. When she stepped into the warm, cheerful kitchen, some of the tenseness, created by thoughts of Sloan, slipped away.

Kendall kissed her grandmother on the cheek, then sat down at the kitchen table. "What would I do without you, Grandma?"

"Learn to cook." Maria Spencer spooned the scrambled eggs onto the plates and set them on the table.

"You know I'm a hopeless case, but you never stop trying."

"You know I'm a stubborn case," Kendall's grandmother retorted, her brown eyes sparkling with mischief, "and I'll never stop trying."

Kendall took several sips of her coffee. "Flora came into the clinic yesterday and she wants me to persuade you to enter your pottery this year."

Maria laughed softly. "Flora has been hounding me for months. Talk about stubborn." She paused, her alert eyes scanning Kendall's face. "You didn't get much sleep last night. You came home late again yesterday. Did you have another emergency?"

Kendall toyed with her piece of toast. "I was delayed at the clinic with a little girl who was bitten by a stray dog."

"I get the feeling there is an 'and' in there somewhere."

"And her father invited me to dinner. I went."

"You did! Are they from around here?" Her grandmother's sharp gaze drilled into her, as though Maria could read what she was thinking.

"No. From St. Louis, on vacation."

"Ah."

There was a wealth of meaning in that one expression, but Maria didn't say anything else while they ate their breakfast. Kendall hadn't dated much since Blake, and when she had, it was only men she had grown up with.

Kendall started to rise and take her dishes to the sink.

"I need to discuss something with you," her grandmother said hesitantly.

Kendall relaxed back in the chair, examining her grandmother's dark features that spoke of her Indian heritage. Kendall was in a hurry, but something in her grandmother's tone conveyed an urgency as well as a reluctance. Studying her across the table, Kendall noted the lines of age in her grandmother's face were deeper, her brown eyes duller. She had been so busy lately that she hadn't noticed the subtle changes in Maria, and Kendall was worried by them.

"I've written my cousin on the reservation in Arizona and expressed a desire to come home."

Shock waves ripped through Kendall. *Home?* "But, Grandma, this is your home!"

"Not really. My heart has always been with my people. I want to die where I was born, on the reservation."

"No! You belong here. You've lived here for over fifty years. You're the only family I have left."

Maria's jaw set in a stubborn line. "I haven't seen my

homeland in twenty years. I want to tie feathers in the wind again. I want to experience again my people's traditions that I've lost sight of here in Spencerville."

Kendall glanced around the kitchen, her thoughts racing wildly in an attempt to make her grandmother understand she needed her. Her gaze rested upon the clock on the wall, and she noticed it was already time for her first appointment.

Kendall rose, her body rigid with indecision. She should stay, but as it was she would be fifteen minutes late for the first patient. "Grandma, I need to be at the clinic. We have to talk about this later. Please don't do anything right now. Family means a lot to me. What would I do if I lost you? You're all I have."

"Kendall, you'll always have my love and support. You'll never lose that, but there will come a day when I will die. Find a man and settle down. Raise your own children. Don't pour all your love into your patients, this town. Leave something for yourself."

All the way to the clinic Kendall was troubled by her grandmother's last words. She didn't want to think about her grandmother dying, or hear it from her. She had always thought of Maria as invincible. Surely she could convince her grandmother to give up the idea of moving back to the Indian reservation in Arizona.

From the moment Kendall arrived at the clinic, she was busy with one patient after another and didn't stop for a coffee break until eleven. She had a few minutes to jot down some notes in a patient's chart before Jackie would be there.

Kendall was raising the coffee cup to her mouth when

the phone rang. Sighing, she placed the cup back down on her desk and answered the phone.

"Dr. Spencer."

"Kendall, this is Sloan."

He didn't need to identify himself; she would have known that voice anywhere. The enticing huskiness of his voice rustled through her, and a vivid mental picture flashed into her mind of their parting the night before.

"The sheriff's office and I have been looking all morning for that dog, but I think he's disappeared off the face of this planet. I think we'd better go ahead and set up an appointment for the first shot. I'll keep looking, but I believe I scared the hell out of that mongrel and he's long gone."

"The vaccine will be here tomorrow morning. Why don't you bring Missi in tomorrow afternoon?"

"Fine. I'm looking forward to seeing you again, even though I wish it were under more pleasant circumstances. Till tomorrow afternoon, then."

Kendall sat for a long time, staring at the phone she had put down. *Looking forward to seeing you* played through her mind over and over. She couldn't deny that she was looking forward to seeing him, too. There was no future, her sensible side declared, but her heart wasn't convinced.

Sloan pulled into the parking lot of the clinic, his hands gripping the steering wheel so tightly that they felt as if they were locked into place. He had kept up a running commentary the whole way to the clinic, but one look at Missi's pale features told him that her mind was still on the rabies shot she was to have. He had brought her asthma medicine, fearing she might have an episode.

"Daddy, I don't want to go in there," Missi said as he turned off the engine.

He faced his daughter, and with relief, took note that her breathing was still even. "Hon, I know you don't, but tomorrow we're going fishing at our special spot we found yesterday." He once again changed the subject quickly before she became worked up.

"May I ask Amy to go with us? I had fun playing with her this morning."

"If you want, hon, that's fine with me." Thank goodness the Frasers rented the cabin next to theirs and had a girl only a year older than Missi. They played together that morning, affording him some more time to look for the dog. He hadn't been successful, though.

"I'll call Amy's parents when we get back home." Sloan climbed out of the car and headed for the clinic, stiff with tension. The next thirty minutes would be difficult. Maybe he should have let Sandra handle this at home. No, Missi was his responsibility, too, and he had to make that clear to Sandra.

When he opened the door and they stepped inside the clinic, Sloan's gaze fastened onto Kendall, standing in the doorway as if she had been waiting for them to arrive. That thought warmed him and made him feel as though he weren't alone.

"Hi, you two," Kendall said, a smile shining in her eyes as they fell upon Sloan's handsome features. Her image of him had been accurate to the smallest detail, she thought with amazement.

Sloan's smile matched hers in brilliance. But in his eyes she saw the troubled look that he was trying to conceal from Missi. He was worried and Kendall wanted to help ease his concern. The urge was strong as she indicated to the pair to follow her into an examination room.

When they were inside room two, Kendall began to understand. Missi was frightened, probably of having a shot, and she would have two of them that afternoon, a gamma globulin and a rabies. Kendall didn't give the girl any time to think, each shot having been prepared right before they arrived. Quickly, before Missi realized what was happening, Kendall gave the child the shots, one right after the other. The whole time she talked with Missi in a low, soothing voice while Sloan helped, sensing that Kendall was trying to get everything over with as swiftly as possible.

Missi's eyes misted, but her breathing increased only slightly as the girl realized everything was over and they hadn't been there three minutes.

"Relax and drink this." Kendall handed Missi a glass of warm water, which would help a person who had asthma breathe easier.

Kendall didn't try to put her arm around Missi's shoulder as she did with other children; but she did smile warmly down at the girl. "Bonnie has a special box where you can pick out a treat to take home with you. You were terrific, Missi."

With shimmering eyes, Missi looked up at her father. "Daddy, can we go now?"

"You need to stay here for fifteen minutes and let me

make sure you're not having a reaction to the vaccine." Kendall moved toward the door. "I have one more patient. Then I'll take a look at your arm."

"Daddy's a doctor. Why can't he look at my arm at home?" Missi's pout turned her mouth downward.

Kendall's face reflected her surprise. "I didn't know," she whispered, glancing toward Sloan and wondering why he had kept that from her.

He grinned broadly. "It's true. I am a doctor of *biochemistry*. Missi, I'm not a doctor of medicine, so I think we'd better leave that to Dr. Spencer."

While Kendall saw her last patient for the day, her thoughts were with Missi and Sloan in the waiting room. One moment she felt as if she had known him all her life, but the next minute, like in the examination room, she realized they were total strangers. She hadn't even known what he did for a living. In fact, she knew very little about the man, except that he was divorced, had a nine-year-old daughter, and lived in St. Louis.

And yet that wasn't completely true, Kendall thought. Through years of working directly with people, she had learned to read them well and quickly. In the short time she had been around Sloan Hunter, she sensed his inner strength, which was tempered with a caring kindness. He would be loyal to a friend, sensitive to another person's needs. There was an air of vigilance about him that Kendall found exciting. She wondered what it would be like if he wasn't in control; he was a man who had complete command of himself.

But what had kept her daydreaming for the past two days was wondering what it would be like if he lost himself in making love, giving totally of himself but taking as well. She kept imagining what his hands and lips would feel like on her body, and even now the thought made her shiver.

Fifteen minutes later, when Kendall entered the waiting room, she couldn't meet Sloan's eyes. Memories of her earlier thoughts caused a blush to stain her cheeks. She hadn't blushed in years!

After examining Missi's arm, Kendall announced, "Everything looks fine. You handled this like a trooper, Missi."

Missi stepped closer to her father, her head down, her gaze glued to the floor. For a brief moment, though, no hostility had flickered in Missi's eyes, which had grown round as Kendall had talked to her.

Sloan's intent regard compelled Kendall to look at him. "We're going to the café. Would you like to join us, Kendall?"

Missi's head shot up, disappointment in her eyes.

Kendall took one look at the young girl. "No, you two go ahead and celebrate. Missi deserves to, but I have work to do at the clinic. I've been so busy lately that I've neglected my charts."

Kendall would like to have gone. She was becoming obsessed with wanting to know everything about Sloan. But even if Missi had wanted her to come, it was best that she didn't. She was diving into the unknown without taking her usual cautious inspection beforehand.

After Sloan and Missi left, Kendall eased down into a chair in the waiting room, trying to bring order to her riotous thoughts. She was torn between wanting to go with him and placing as much distance as possible between them. The situation was dangerous to her emotional state, she decided. But still . . .

"I'm leaving, Kendall," Bonnie said from the doorway.

Kendall's head jerked up. "Going? Oh, yes, see you tomorrow."

"He sure is handsome."

"Who?"

"You know who, Kendall Spencer. I've seen you look at him, and Jackie told me you two had dinner the other night at the café."

"With his daughter." Kendall stood. "Aren't there any secrets in this town?"

"No. You know your life is an open book. Most of the people know what you're doing before you do."

Kendall rolled her shoulders, kneading the knotted cords of her neck. "Well, you can put a stop to any rumors flying around Spencerville about me and the stranger. I won't be running off to St. Louis tomorrow."

"How about in five weeks?"

Kendall gasped as she twisted about to stare at her friend. "Bonnie!"

An impish grin was plastered all over Bonnie's face as she held up both of her hands. "Just kidding. You wouldn't do anything impulsive like that!"

Kendall walked past Bonnie toward her office, saying over her shoulder, "Didn't you say you were leaving?"

But Bonnie followed Kendall into her office and waited until Kendall was seated behind her desk before asking, "Why didn't you go to dinner with him? Not many men like that one around Spencerville." Bonnie angled her head, tapping a finger against her chin. "In fact, I can't think of one."

"Go home to Kirk, Bonnie. I have work to do and I don't need to waste my time talking about Sloan." Weariness laced her voice.

"Okay. I can take a hint. But you work way too hard and never go out. At least when you were dating Blake . . ."

"Don't bring him into this. As you pointed out, there aren't too many choices in Spencerville."

"That's why you should . . ."

"Good night!" Exasperation edged its way into Kendall's features as she picked up her black fountain pen and began to write.

Kendall was relieved when she heard the door close and the office became quiet, a soothing balm after the long day. She hadn't realized how tensed she had been, waiting for Sloan to arrive, until after he had left. When he had walked out the door, it had been as if her bones and muscles had liquefied.

Staring down at the chart before her, Kendall couldn't think of anything to write in it. Even though she knew she should work, her mind was filled with Sloan Hunter and the look of promise he had given her that evening in the café parking lot. Maybe something could come of getting to know him. *No, Kendall Spencer, you are only fooling yourself if you believe that one.* She would be hurt, perhaps, but that would be all.

Kendall flipped the chart closed and stood, all in one motion. It would be useless to kid herself about working.

She knew she couldn't after her encounter with Sloan. Besides, she was tired and needed a better night's sleep than she had been getting lately.

Kendall quickly gathered up her purse and medical bag and left the clinic. When she stepped into her house, the smells of dinner wafted to her and she headed straight for the kitchen.

"I'm sure hungry and it smells delicious, Grandma." Kendall placed her purse and bag on the counter, then lifted a pan top to peer inside. "Mmm. Fresh asparagus from your garden. You know how to get to my heart fast. Through my stomach."

"Never could say you're one of those girls who diets all the time."

"One of the hazards of my profession. I'm always on the go, burning up those calories."

"Well, sit. It's ready. And you can tell me over dinner what has you all riled up."

Kendall shot her grandmother a quick glance. "I'm not all riled up."

Maria chuckled as she carried the plates to the table. "You're talking to the woman who raised you."

"Then why do you have it in your head to go back to the reservation?"

"And don't think you can use that old ploy and change the subject on me. It's that man with the little girl who was bitten." There was no curiosity behind the flat statement, as though her grandmother already knew everything.

Sometimes Kendall couldn't help but think her grandmother was a clairvoyant. While she had been growing up, she had never been able to hide anything from Maria, so at a young age, she had learned to be honest and direct.

"Yes. I'm attracted to Sloan Hunter, but there are problems."

"One being he isn't from around here."

Kendall nodded, toying with her food, her appetite gone. "I would say that's a pretty big reason not to become involved."

"Kendall, you think too much of the future. Let the future take care of itself. If something feels right for today, don't worry about what might happen later."

Maria never lectured. She might say one or two things. Then she would become silent and allow Kendall to think. The rest of the dinner was finished in silence. Then Maria rushed Kendall out of the kitchen and told her to relax in the den with a good book. Kendall could do neither. She prowled restlessly about the room, having ten minutes before placed the book she had picked out back in the bookcase.

When the phone rang, Kendall jumped, motionless for a few seconds. "I'll get it," she shouted.

When she heard his deep, husky voice, her heartbeat quickened, and her legs refused to support her. She sank down onto a chair by the phone.

"The neighbors next door want Missi to go with them tomorrow afternoon to an amusement park near Little Rock. She'll be gone until after dinner. That leaves me alone in a strange town with nothing to do. What about taking pity on a stranger and going with him on a picnic?"

If it feels right, do it. And this definitely feels right,
Kendall thought. "I'd love to. I'll be through with my
last patient at five."

"I'll pick you up at six at your place. Where is it?"

After giving him her address, Kendall questioned him
about how Missi was doing before they said good-bye.
She struggled to make her voice sound neutral while
discussing Missi, but Kendall was worried about the
next shot. The child's fear of shots and her asthma could
make the situation explosive. As she turned away from
the phone, Kendall decided she would have to be
prepared for the worst.

And could she prepare herself for the worst with
Sloan? Because she realized she intended to see him
while he was vacationing on Crystal Lake. This time she
wouldn't think beyond five weeks.

Chapter Four

$\mathcal{K}$ endall flew into the house and headed straight for her bedroom. She had only ten minutes to get ready for the picnic, having been held up at the clinic by the last patient. Tearing off her clothes, she quickly showered, then dressed in a pair of jeans and a red T-shirt. After slipping on her sandals and freshening up her makeup, she walked from her bedroom, toward the voices she heard in the kitchen.

Sloan and her grandmother were seated at the kitchen table, drinking a glass of iced tea. A warm feeling of family engulfed Kendall as she watched them from the doorway. Sloan, sensing her presence, twisted about and welcomed her with a smile that crinkled the corners of his night-dark eyes.

"We were comparing notes about Arizona," Sloan explained as Kendall advanced into the room.

"A lot has changed since I last saw home." Maria's brown eyes had a faraway look in them.

Home? There's that word again, Kendall thought, apprehensive. She sat across from Sloan, wanting to question her grandmother further about the usage of the word "home." But her grandmother would never discuss it in front of a stranger. She would wait and talk with her grandmother later that evening.

"A research institute in Phoenix a year ago flew me out there and gave me the grand tour of the area. Beautiful. The desert was in bloom and the view was breathtaking. I was very tempted to take their job offer."

"Why didn't you take it?" Kendall asked, her eyes traveling from his ruggedly handsome features to his knit shirt, enticingly stretched across his broad chest.

"I still have about two years to go on the project I'm working on now at the university. I couldn't leave it in the middle."

Kendall was about to question him further on his research project, but her grandmother interrupted. "You two go ahead and run along. Flora is coming over tonight to try to convince me to enter the fair." Maria stood, chuckling. "No wonder the fair is such a success every year. That woman doesn't know how to take the word 'no.'"

When they stepped outside onto the front porch, she breathed deeply of the grass, the flowers, the moisture-laden air. Kendall hadn't taken the time recently to enjoy an evening with a light breeze scenting the air with smells of summer. She felt totally relaxed in Sloan's presence, which surprised her. The memory of his warm smile, earlier in the kitchen, erased any tension she had. She was strangely excited at the prospect of spending a few hours alone with him.

"Your grandmother is quite a lady." Sloan opened the door to his sports car.

"She's been the backbone of this town for a long time. But it wasn't easy for her at first. The townspeople didn't welcome her because she was a stranger and an Indian. But my father used to tell me about how she won their hearts one by one. She meets a challenge head on."

"Like Flora." Sloan slid into the driver's seat and started the car.

A soft laugh rippled from Kendall's throat. "Yes, like Flora. I hope you and Missi will be here for the fair on the Fourth of July."

He looked sidelong at her, his eyes gleaming. "We wouldn't miss the most important event around here, especially when I hear you are the county's champion three-legged racer."

"Who did you hear that from?"

"It's common knowledge." Golden sparks of humor glowed in his eyes as his gaze strayed to her again, skimming over her features, then down the length of her. "I was just trying to imagine you in a potato sack, hopping over the finish line. Do you have a partner yet for this year?"

"No—and answer my question, Sloan Hunter. Who's been talking?"

"Bonnie. Now you answer my question. Can I be your partner in the race? I've never been to a county fair."

"This isn't exactly a county fair." Kendall paused and scanned the lake area they were passing. "Where are we going?"

"Your grandmother told me about a cove on the other side of the lake. It sounded nice, so we're heading there."

And very private, Kendall added to herself. It was a favorite place of her grandmother's, one Maria had shared only with her husband and family. What was her grandmother trying to do? Match-make? Maria Spencer hadn't liked Blake, but on her first meeting with Sloan Hunter she had told him about the cove. What was it about the man that warmed people to him immediately? But the answer to that question came instantly into Kendall's mind. He was charming, friendly, sensitive, but mostly he cared about people, and it showed in his attitude.

When he pulled to a stop near the cove, Sloan twisted about in the car and faced her, his smile sudden and beguiling. "You must have a favorite partner and don't want to hurt my feelings. Give it to me straight. I'm tough, Kendall. Do I have to find someone else?"

"And have you racing against me? No way, Sloan. You got yourself a partner."

Sloan reached behind his seat and took a picnic basket out, then climbed from the car. When Kendall stood, he offered his hand in invitation and hers slipped into his large grasp, his fingers settling pleasantly about hers.

They walked down toward the lake together. "Missi's looking forward to the fair," Sloan said. "The girl next door comes to Crystal Lake every year and has been telling Missi how much fun the fair is."

"How long has Missi had asthma?" Kendall felt Sloan tense as his fingers tightened about her hand.

"Most of her life. But it has become worse in the last year since the divorce. In fact, she had to be hospitalized once."

"Has Missi had any counseling?"

"No. I know asthma can be aggravated by emotional problems sometimes, but she doesn't live with me. I see her at Christmas and in the summer. There's not much time to build a good relationship."

There was a hint of sharpness in his voice that caused Kendall to stop and turn toward him. "She feels threatened right now by the change, by the fact that she doesn't see you very much."

The taut lines in his face gradually faded. "I know. Her mother wanted Missi to come home right after the dog bit her. But I'm very determined to establish a few things now at the beginning—first, that Missi and I will have this time every year, and second, that I am Missi's father and therefore have some rights, too." His voice softened as he spoke.

Sloan lifted his free hand and touched Kendall's cheek with the back of it. All thoughts of anything except the two of them suddenly shattered like a smashed windshield. Then gently he took a strand of her hair and wound it loosely about a finger, staring deeply into her eyes.

"You are beautiful," he said huskily, finally letting

the strand of hair drop back into place as he broke the visual link with her and stepped away.

Her throat felt tight, her pulse hammering against her temples. For an instant Kendall wanted to say the hell with the picnic and getting to know him. She wanted his arms about her, his mouth kissing hers. The sudden silence between them heightened her sexual awareness of Sloan as he spread a blanket on the carpet of grass and delved into the basket.

Kendall blinked and sat on the blanket, forcing a lightness into her voice. "I'm starved." She appraised the array of food before her and added, "I thought you said you couldn't cook. This looks good."

He grinned a positively devilish grin as he poured two glasses of red wine and handed one to Kendall. "I cannot tell a lie. I had this catered."

"Catered! A picnic!"

"I didn't want to take any chances that I might blow it, so I went to the café and ordered this food. I wanted our first date, alone, to be perfect."

There was a sensual suggestiveness in his voice that sent her heart beating wildly against her breast. The heat of his gaze boldly surveyed her face, watching for her reaction. His roguish grin widened as he turned his attention to preparing the smoked ham, various cheeses, freshly baked bread and strawberries and whipped cream.

"Have you always practiced in Spencerville?" Sloan asked as he laid a plate in front of her.

"Yes, except for my internship and residency at a hospital in Little Rock. Ever since I can remember it was expected of me to go to medical school, then return to Spencerville and take up practice with my father.''

Sloan tore his piece of bread in half. ''And how did you feel about those plans?''

Kendall tilted her head to one side, surprise in her expression. ''I never really thought about it. It was just a fact I grew up with and never questioned. Traditionally, a Spencer has always been the doctor here. I love being a doctor, so everything has worked out fine.''

''Yes, if that was what you really wanted. Traditions can sometimes trap a person, though, because they haven't changed with the times and allowed for the differences in a person.''

''Traditions are important, Sloan. Our lives are full of them, like at Christmas.''

''But they aren't written in stone, never to be changed.'' Sloan took several sips of his wine, wondering why suddenly it had been important to make his point. In the short time he had known Kendall he had sensed a part of her was held in reserve, as though she denied her wants to herself. ''Tell me some more about Spencerville,'' he commanded gently, wanting to know all about the town that tied Kendall to it.

While they ate, Kendall told him about the town and some of the interesting people who lived in Spencerville, with each question that Sloan asked probing deeper into Kendall's life. By the time she finished her ham and cheese, she realized he had told her absolutely nothing about himself.

Reclining back on one elbow, she toyed with a strawberry in the whipped cream, saying in a flippant voice, "Are you practicing to be a man of mystery? You have said very little about yourself. I know you live in St. Louis, worked at a university on a research project and have a little girl named Missi. But that certainly can't be all."

"But aren't you supposed to let the other person talk about herself?" Sloan leaned over and took the strawberry from her fingers, swirling it around in the cream, then offering it to her.

Their gazes locked as she bent forward slightly to take a bite of the strawberry. They remained invisibly bound as he wiped a trace of whipped cream from her mouth with his thumb, then sucked it off, titillating thoughts shimmering in his eyes.

"What kind of project do you work on?" Her question came out on a breathless rush of air.

"I'm involved in lung cancer research." He dipped another strawberry into the whipped cream and raised it to her mouth, his actions captivating her full attention.

For the life of her she couldn't think of another question to ask him, not when he was regarding her with such an intense, enthralling look, not when his finger was outlining her lips with a soft touch, and not when her skin felt so feverish.

Slow down, Kendall, she told herself, bolting upright, severing the hypnotic spell she felt encasing her in his potent power.

"This is the prettiest time of day, when the sun begins to set over the lake." She began to chat about the times she would come out to the lake and swim right before dusk or fish on the bank.

Kendall sat on the blanket with her knees drawn up, her arms about her legs, as she realized he hadn't spoken a word. She fell silent, staring out across the lake. Her gaze drifted upward to where the dying sun tinted the horizon above the trees a vivid red-orange, pinks and mauves edging the sunset in the darkening sky, all the bright colors mirrored in the waters beyond her like glimmering liquid fire.

"Do you like your job, Sloan?" Suddenly she needed to know everything about him. As she watched the sun descend in the sky, she acknowledged to herself that there was no turning back with Sloan, that something had begun that evening between them and they would see it through to the end. The thought of things ending between them before they had really even started sliced her heart in two.

"Yes, very much. It was what kept me going during my divorce and afterward. When Sandra took Missi away from St. Louis to live in Atlanta, I realized how lonely my life was without my daughter. More and more I began to dread coming home every night to an empty house."

His hand brushed down her arm so lightly she wasn't even sure if he had touched her, except that his nearness was vital and compelling, drawing her into his sphere with merely one thrilling touch. It ignited a primitive response inside her, his unmistakable desire commanding and aggressive. She let herself be absorbed by his raw masculinity, which was reaching out and laying claim to her.

"I want you, Kendall. The first day I saw you at the

clinic I knew it, and I think you felt it, too. For the last few days you're about all I can think of."

His voice was rough with longing as his thumb stroked her earlobe, as though he had always known the one place that could stir her beyond logical thinking more than any other sensitive area. It was her Achilles' heel, and he had immediately homed in on it.

She shifted on the blanket, her arms dropping away from around her legs as she dragged a shaky hand through her mass of black curls. The steady, rhythmic sound of the waves disguised the slight tremor in her voice as she whispered, "Yes."

She remained quiet, her eyes on the treetops where the sun had disappeared. Dusk settled around them like a warm blanket that was familiar and comfortable.

His mouth nibbled her earlobe, then grazed a path of fire down her neck with a sensual ease that shook her to her core. Then suddenly his mouth was no longer caressing her. She twisted about to look at him, lying back on the blanket, with the smoldering embers of his black eyes scorching her resistance. He held a hand up, silently inviting her into the shelter of his arms.

For a brief moment a battle warred within her, but the impulse to bridge the distance between them was too strong. She fitted her hand within his, and he hauled her against his whipcord strength, tangling his fingers in her hair, combing it away from her face as he crushed his lips onto hers with an urgency that had been held in check for too long, but suddenly allowed its freedom.

Sloan parted her lips swiftly and proceeded to plunder her mouth with a strange mixture of tenderness and roughness. She gloried in his hunger for her, in the searing domination of his tongue searching the hidden recesses of her mouth. He made her feel womanly, desired, washing away some of the doubts that Blake's accusations had created in her.

His mouth was warm, firm and persuasive as it traveled over her face, trailing light, burning kisses to her earlobe. While he nipped at it lovingly, his hand tugged her T-shirt from her waistband, then moved under and up to cup her breast. A wild quiver of excitement gripped her as his strong, lean fingers spread wide, his palm circling each breast. Rolling each nipple between his thumb and forefinger, they hardened into peaks of excruciating pleasure.

With a moan he ravaged her mouth again, bathing her in a fierce all-consuming need. His seduction was elemental and overpowering, and Kendall struggled to retain control. Suddenly everything was moving too fast for her. She hadn't had time to think this through.

As they had talked earlier, she had been struck with the realization that she had wanted more from Sloan than a month-long affair. But that realization now was coupled with the fact there could be nothing but a brief affair between them.

When his hand stroked back and forth across her breasts, then roamed lower over her stomach to the snap of her jeans, her common sense finally surfaced, and she wedged her arms between them.

"No, this isn't right," she murmured. "We can't."

The feel of his mahogany-dark eyes on her in disbelief made her heart beat even faster. She could hear his breath struggling in his throat; she could see him fighting for control.

"Not right? What kind of game are you playing with me, Kendall?" Sloan asked in a dangerously even voice.

"I don't play games." Kendall smoothed her T-shirt back into place and moved away from him, his tantalizing closeness too much for her to handle in her present disconcerted state.

The full impact of his anger was directed at her as he asked in frustration, "Then what do you call what you just did?"

"I call it coming to my senses before things get carried away and we start something that can have only one ending." Kendall shot to her feet and rapidly put some distance between them.

At the edge of the lake Kendall stared out at the growing darkness, the moonlight shimmering on the water in silvery radiance. She tried to marshal her own anger, but she couldn't because she had been wrong. Conflicting emotions were tearing her apart. She couldn't change overnight. Concern about her future was still too important to her to disregard, even though the moment felt so right.

Sloan's hands lay heavily upon her shoulders, and he pulled her back against him. "You're right, Kendall. I was moving too fast with you. But I have no intention of completely retreating. What's between us has already reached the point of no return. I want to get to know *everything* about you."

His whispered words disarmed her, and she snuggled against him, suddenly elated that he wasn't angry anymore and that he did understand. For a long time they stood on the shore, his arms wrapped around her, her head resting on his shoulder.

"Let's walk a little bit," Sloan finally murmured against her ear, stirring her hair, tingling her neck.

His arm went about her, drawing her close as they strolled along the lake's edge in silence. The companionship she felt with Sloan in those precious moments was like nothing she had ever experienced before, and she could only marvel at the feelings he was provoking in her—feelings of being needed as a woman, not just a doctor, feelings of being desired, of being in complete accord with another human being.

"I want Missi to get to know you, Kendall." Sloan paused and turned her to face him, tilting her chin up to move his mouth across hers.

"But, Sloan . . ."

He stilled the rest of her sentence with a kiss of fire and desperation, his hands pressing her closer to him. When they parted, his quick intake of air, the intensity in his features conveyed the fascination they felt for each other, as if everything was out of their control.

"No buts, Kendall. I know Missi feels threatened by you. Let's face it. We haven't exactly kept it a secret we're attracted to each other," Sloan said dryly as he coiled an arm about her shoulder and they started back toward the blanket. "Missi has to realize that I'll always love her, but I do have a life of my own. This vacation is important to Missi, but I want you to be a part of us, too."

At the picnic spot, Kendall picked up the blanket and

folded it while Sloan packed the basket. She had to get away from him to think, put some order back into her life.

"Missi and you must have time alone," Kendall finally said.

"I know. But, Kendall, until I met you I didn't realize how lonely I really was. I want to be with you all the time, which I know isn't possible." Sloan folded her against him, his arms a tender band about her. "But I don't know why I can't see you and still give Missi the attention she needs. Things usually have a way of working out."

He kissed her lightly on the lips, then again and again until, laughing, Kendall pulled away from him. "I think we'd better be heading back. Missi will be returning home soon and I have a long day tomorrow."

"Are you always so practical and realistic?" Sloan asked as they walked up the slope to his sports car.

"Always." *Well, almost always,* she amended to herself. *Around you I find it very hard to be practical. And what's realistic about our situation?*

"I think I'd better stop by the cabin to make sure Missi isn't back. You're right about its being late," Sloan said as he started the car.

He drove by the Frasers' cabin, but there were no lights on inside. When he pulled onto the gravel road that led to his place, he stopped halfway to the cabin, his headlights illuminating the road and a mangy-looking dog by the side.

"It's that damned dog," he muttered between clenched teeth, slamming the car into Park.

Sloan jerked the door open and was swiftly out of the car. "Be careful, Sloan," Kendall yelled after him.

The stray dog growled and backed away. Sloan picked up a large stick and headed around the front of the car. The dog's eyes glowed in the headlights, and Kendall shuddered. Fear constricted her throat and twisted a huge knot in her stomach.

Against her better judgment, she opened the car door and climbed out, her fingers clutching the door frame in a viselike hold.

Sloan had halted, appraising the situation and trying to decide the best way to capture the dog when he heard the car door open. "Get back into that car immediately."

His voice was a low growl, as menacing as the dog's. Kendall started to protest that she could help when he added in a lethally quiet voice, "I don't want to have to worry about you, too."

The dog's eyes darted from one person to the other. Then it turned and scurried away into the underbrush. The rustle of the leaves disturbed the stillness. Then the silence once again reigned.

"Dammit! I'll get that dog yet." Sloan was beside her in three stiff strides, his hand clamping around her wrist in a bruising grip. "Why in the hell didn't you stay in the car?" Frustration and anger contorted his features into an angry mask.

"I wanted to help," Kendall managed to say, impaled beneath his icy stare that immobilized her with its calculating coldness.

"I might have had a chance, one on one with him." Tension throbbed in her temples and her own anger stirred inside her. "Oh, sure. I would have ended up with two patients instead of one," she said in a mocking voice.

"Get into the car. I'll have to call the sheriff's office to let him know the dog is still in the neighborhood."

With a quick downward motion, Kendall yanked her wrist from his grasp and slid back into the car. They lapsed into a smoldering silence the rest of the way to the cabin.

Inside Sloan poured himself a drink of whiskey and bolted it down as he walked into the kitchen to call the sheriff. Kendall stood just inside the doorway, undecided on what she should do when Sloan reappeared. His face was set in grim lines as he placed his empty glass on a table, then raked his fingers through his hair.

While Kendall watched Sloan trying to calm his raging emotion, sparked by the dog's appearance and her impulsive actions, recent memories of his kisses returned to confuse her. They had been enticing, teasing, devastating as they had urged her to surrender to his powerful domination, exerted so effortlessly over her.

She wanted to cross the short space between them and smooth away the frustration he felt, the helplessness this situation with Missi created, but she stood immobile by the front door, unsure. His anxiety twisted inside of him, and affected her, too. Finally, she couldn't remain by the door any longer.

Quickly she covered the few feet and touched his face. Her soft gray eyes reflected the concern written in her features as her fingertips grazed his jaw, compelling him to look directly into her face.

He cupped her hand and held it to his face, his eyes velvet brown. She felt the tautness in his jaw fade; she saw the hardness in his expression soften. He pulled her close to him and buried his face in the ebony strands of her hair.

"I'm sorry I snapped at you. If I ever get my hands on that damned dog, I'll strangle it for what it put Missi through." He drew slightly away, but his arms were still about her. "I'm dreading this next shot, Kendall. And Kirk said he couldn't have any men out here until tomorrow morning. I've already been through this before. The dog will be gone by then." A weary defeat made his voice raw.

He regarded her with an unwavering absorption for a long moment. Slowly his mouth descended toward hers, his liquid eyes melting her resolve to put a rational distance between them. His lips were a breath away when the slamming of a car door disturbed the night and parted them.

Sloan strode toward the door and swung it open as Ed Fraser was about to knock. Missi and her girl friend were standing next to him. Kendall responded with all the correct, polite phrases when Sloan introduced her to his neighbor, but all the while she was forcing her pulse to beat at a slower, safer rate.

When Kendall's senses were no longer clamoring for the feel of Sloan's lips on hers, her attention was fixed upon Missi, who was very quiet and withdrawn while Sloan escorted Ed and Amy Fraser to their car.

"How was the amusement park, Missi?" Kendall asked.

"Okay," the little girl finally answered after a long pause. "Why are you here?"

"Because I asked her," Sloan said from the doorway, his tone firm, his look steady. "We need to take Kendall home. Let's go."

Kendall was relieved when Sloan parked his car in her driveway. The disquieting silence in the car, even when Sloan had tried to draw Missi out about the amusement park, only re-enforced the problems that stood between Kendall and him.

"I'll be right back, Missi. I'm going to walk Kendall to the door."

"No." Kendall practically shouted the word. "I'll manage," she murmured quickly, then yanked the door open and fled the small, stifling confines of the car.

Kendall didn't release her trapped breath until she was inside her house and leaning against the wood. The sound of Sloan's car leaving deluged her with mixed feelings. *Oh, my God, I want him!* But in her mind and heart she couldn't see a future for them beyond the next month.

"Kendall, is that you?" her grandmother called out from her bedroom.

With the sound of her grandmother's voice, Kendall suddenly remembered something else she had to handle that evening. Squaring her shoulders, she strode into her grandmother's bedroom to find out about the letter Maria had written to her cousin on the reservation.

"How was the evening?" Maria's shrewd eyes took in the strained look on Kendall's face.

Kendall didn't answer the question. "Are you really

thinking about going back to Arizona?'' she asked instead.

"Yes. I have been for several months, and last week I finally wrote Anna. If she has a place for me, I'll be leaving soon.''

Wearily, Kendall sank down on her grandmother's bed. "You can't!''

"I've lived in Spencerville most of my life. First, because your grandfather had his practice here, even though I hated leaving my people. And second, because of you. After your mother died in childbirth, you needed someone to raise you and I wanted to. Now it's my turn to do something for myself. I will go if my cousin wants me.''

Kendall heard the determination in her grandmother's voice and knew she couldn't talk her out of her decision. She had no right to ask her grandmother to stay any longer in Spencerville. Her shoulders sagged with that thought as Kendall shoved herself from the bed and headed for her own bedroom.

In one short week her whole life had turned upside down, her emotions tattered and shredded into hundreds of pieces. She was strongly attracted to a man who was all wrong for her, and her grandmother would be leaving soon. What was happening to the logical, controlled woman she had always been? She had never allowed her emotions to rule her life or her decisions. They couldn't if she was to be an effective doctor. But yet, lately that seemed to be all she was doing—listening to her heart.

Chapter Five

$\mathcal{K}$ endall stood at the window in her office with her hands clasped behind her back. Sloan and Missi would be there in a few minutes and she still hadn't decided what to do about Sloan. The past two days since the picnic her thoughts had been filled with him. A vague dissatisfied restlessness prevailed her every awakened moment.

"Damn him for disrupting my life like this," Kendall muttered, turning away from the window and walking toward the door.

Since the picnic they had talked only once briefly on the phone, but she kept telling herself that Sloan was busy scouring the area for the dog or spending time with Missi. Kendall missed him, though, and hated this growing dependency.

As she entered the waiting room, the outer door to the

clinic opened and Sloan and Missi walked inside. Kendall's attention immediately flew to Missi, who was unusually pale and anxious.

Swiftly Kendall crossed the room, noting with a quick glimpse toward Sloan the worried expression on his face, his dark eyes clouded with a mounting concern. Kneeling down in front of Missi, Kendall smiled, fixing the young girl's gaze on her. Missi's nostrils were flared as she tried to inhale and her breathing was becoming fast. These early warning signs alerted Kendall to a possible asthma episode, and she knew she needed to act quickly, but calmly and reassuringly.

"I've been looking forward all day to seeing you, Missi. I wanted to know who got the biggest fish yesterday." While Kendall spoke in a soothing voice, she was guiding Missi into room one and helping her to lie down.

"I want you to relax, Missi. Good. Now, I want you to drink this water. Do you have any breathing exercises?" Kendall asked gently.

Missi nodded, the frightened look easing as she listened to Kendall's reassuring voice, which was soft but firm, as though there were nothing wrong.

Sloan held out Missi's medicine, which Kendall took and gave to Missi, saying, "Take this. That's good."

While Sloan held Missi's hand, he watched Kendall, a deep feeling of admiration for her growing in him. Sandra, when trying to cope with Missi, had always been anxious and worried, or at times when Missi had done something to aggravate the asthma, she berated Missi for her foolishness. For the first time he saw that

Missi was really listening, her attention directed at Kendall and not upon her difficulty with breathing. This feat, accomplished by Kendall's calm actions, caused the tenseness to fade in Missi's expression, her hard breathing to lessen some.

An hour later with Missi relaxed and as she was breathing deeply and evenly, Kendall gave her the rabies shot, explaining the importance of the shot to Missi, talking to her as if she were an adult and capable of handling the situation.

"You have a right to know and you're old enough to understand the necessity of the shots, even though I know you don't like it. Do you know there's a boy here in Spencerville that I'd like you to meet? He has asthma just like you." Kendall leaned against the table, a warmth radiating from her as she went on to tell Missi about Chris.

By the time the fifteen minutes were up and Kendall checked Missi's arm for any allergic reaction, everything was normal again.

"Daddy, when can I meet Chris? He's been in a swim meet. Gosh, would I like to learn how to swim!"

"Any time is fine with me, hon." The tense concern was completely gone from his expression, relief shining in his eyes.

Sloan glanced up and trapped Kendall within the intently probing depths of his eyes. In his look, Kendall saw his appreciation, which went beyond what she had done for Missi.

"I could probably arrange something for tomorrow," Kendall said slowly, dragging her gaze away from

Sloan's and busying herself by putting away her equipment, since Missi was the last patient for the day. For just an instant, nothing else had mattered except Sloan. He had a way of wiping away reality and focusing all her attention on him alone.

"I'd like that." Missi dropped her gaze to her lap, her hands twisting together. "Uh . . . Daddy and . . . I wanted to know if you'd have dinner at the cabin with us tonight," she finally said, as though she had rehearsed the invitation many times.

Kendall shot Sloan a questioning look. After Missi's close call she didn't want to put any more strain on the situation. Yet it wasn't good to let a child with asthma feel that she could manipulate people at her will.

One corner of his mouth lifted in a crooked grin. "I thought three bad cooks somehow could manage to fix an edible dinner."

"You're a dreamer, Sloan Hunter. All that crazy logic will succeed in getting you is one awful dinner and three starving people. I've got a better idea based on a sound principle. You two are invited to eat at my house. My grandmother is one of the best cooks in the county, probably in the whole state of Arkansas."

"We couldn't impose, Kendall."

"You don't know my grandmother. She always fixes enough for anyone in Spencerville who might just happen to drop by about supper time. Besides, I'll call Chris and we'll see if we can set up something for tomorrow." *Oh, my Lord, I actually sound like I'm bribing Missi. Am I that desperate to see Sloan?*

Sloan glanced down at Missi, his half-grin unfolding

into a radiant smile that charmed Kendall and produced an increase in her heart rate.

"Well, it looks like we have this evening taken care of. But Missi, what do you figure we can do about tomorrow night? Throw ourselves on Kendall's grandmother's mercy this evening?"

"Oh, Daddy!" Missi exclaimed, laughter tinging her voice.

Kendall liked the sound of Missi's laughter, but she had a feeling the little girl didn't laugh as much as she should. "I have a couple of things to finish up, but it will only take a few minutes. Then you two can follow me to my house."

In her office Kendall made two calls, first to a patient, then to her grandmother to tell her Sloan and Missi would be joining them for dinner. Then she quickly checked her appearance in a mirror, running a comb through her black curls, and putting some lipstick on.

She was thirty-two years old and had allowed only one man, Blake, to get close to her, and that relationship had ended badly. Blake and she had had a lot in common, but things hadn't worked out for them. Now she was contemplating becoming involved with a man who would be in Spencerville for only a month more and she doubted they even had much in common. The point was that she didn't know and suddenly she found herself not caring! The feelings he provoked in her were new and ecstatic, and she wanted to explore these new sensations to the fullest.

All the way to her house Kendall, though, tried to place a tight rein on the happy feelings bubbling inside her. She started reviewing, again, the reasons it wouldn't work between them, but she couldn't get past the first one. Her grandmother was always telling her to take life one day at a time, to enjoy the moment and not always to rationalize, organize and plan the future. So, for the evening she would!

Kendall waited on the porch for Sloan and Missi. His tight-fitting jeans hugged the corded muscles of his legs while his navy-blue knit shirt revealed a broad chest, communicating the power of the man. His strides were fluid, his self-confidence transmitted in every movement of his body. An easy smile descended over his features as he mounted the steps to the front porch.

"I believe we have reservations for two," Sloan quipped, his infectious grin very contagious as it encompassed his whole face. "This restaurant comes highly recommended."

"Follow me, sir, mademoiselle. Your table isn't quite ready." Kendall opened the front door and stood aside, gesturing grandly for Sloan and Missi to go ahead of her.

An odd expression flitted across Missi's face as she looked from Kendall to her father. The pout was gone, though. Hope had been planted in Kendall earlier at the clinic when Missi hadn't completely withdrawn from her even after the young girl had calmed down. Kendall sensed that Missi had always been very frightened when an asthma episode had started, which had aggravated the situation even more.

Maria Spencer entered the living room from the kitchen, wiping her hands on an apron, a broad smile of welcome on her face.

"I've heard so much about you, Missi, from Kendall." The genuine warmth emanating from Maria was a tangible force as she crossed the room to introduce herself and to shake hands with Sloan and Missi. Earlier on the phone, Kendall had briefly told Maria about some of the circumstances that had led to Missi and Sloan's coming to dinner.

There was a twinkle in Maria's dark eyes as they took in Sloan. Her curiosity was definitely aroused since Kendall never brought anyone home for dinner. Not even Blake. Somehow Kendall had known Blake would prefer eating at an expensive restaurant.

"It's not easy having to go through the rabies shots," Maria continued in a soft voice. "Would you like to give me a hand out in the kitchen, Missi? I've never been to Atlanta and would love to hear about it."

In a few short sentences her grandmother had captivated Missi's heart, Kendall realized as she read the expression on Missi's face. Maria had complimented her, asked for the girl's help, then adeptly changed the subject to a safe one.

Kendall watched the two leave the living room, a frown creasing her brow. Why couldn't the situation between her and Missi be that simple and relaxed?

A pair of muscular arms slid around Kendall and pulled her back against a solid wall of male power. "Your grandmother isn't a threat to Missi," Sloan whispered in a husky tone, his warm breath fanning her neck and sending shivers cascading over her.

For just a moment Kendall allowed herself to lean into his strength, reveling in the secure feel of his arms about her middle. There were many thoughts swirling about in Kendall's mind that she wanted to say in that moment.

Will there be anything between us that will make Missi see me as a threat?

I'm not a threat because you'll be leaving in a month.

Oh, how I would love to allow myself not to worry about what might happen in the future.

Maybe things could work out between us.

Am I brave enough to find out?

But she voiced none of those thoughts. Instead, she closed her eyes for a brief moment and transported herself and Sloan to a deserted island where the surf pounded the beach and the sun bathed their naked bodies in golden glory.

"Mmm. You have a distinctive scent, lady." His voice was a low growl that rippled over her in seductive waves. "Violets and alcohol. I don't believe I know that perfume."

"And you, sir, know how to diffuse a romantic moment with only a few words."

Kendall wiggled free of his embrace and faced him, her hands on her waist as though his teasing words had really hurt her. In truth, she liked the idea that he felt he could kid her. Her life had always been so serious, almost as though everything were life and death.

"Dinner is served," Missi announced from the doorway.

"Saved by the bell, woman," Sloan retorted lightly in a whisper. "Or I would have demonstrated how quickly that fuse could be rekindled—with only *one* action."

"Promises, promises," Kendall returned in a teasing voice as she sauntered past him into the kitchen.

At the kitchen table Kendall sat across from Sloan, their eyes continually seeking each other as the dinner progressed. Kendall found it hard to concentrate on eating the mutton loaf, a favorite of hers, or the Indian fry bread, sweetened and drenched in honey. Usually she ate a big meal at night since she rarely had time during the day to sit down and eat much. But Sloan's teasing manner in the living room and the disarming looks he was giving her were eroding her composure, robbing her of her appetite.

Determinedly Kendall looked away from Sloan and spoke to Missi. "After dinner I'll call Chris. In the summer he's usually at the local swimming pool until dark. Ever since Chris discovered swimming, that's about the only place you find him during the day."

Kendall knew she was chatting on and on because she felt uncomfortable with Sloan staring at her, and she knew he was staring at her. She felt it in every fiber of her being, as if he were touching her with his hands instead of his gaze.

"I wish I could learn. Mommy told me I couldn't because of my asthma. She won't let me do anything, while the other kids get to do everything."

The pout had returned to Missi's face, but this time Kendall sensed it wasn't directed at her. Missi felt trapped by her asthma, unable to do what other children her age were doing. Kendall's eyes fastened onto Sloan's troubled ones. His jaw clenched; his shoulders were rigidly set. She wondered if the asthma had been a sore subject with him and his wife.

Kendall quickly searched for a different topic of conversation, but her thoughts were riveted upon Sloan. She couldn't think of a thing to say!

Maria handed the plate with the bread on it to Missi, saying, "When Kendall called and told me you were coming I decided to fix some Indian fry bread. When I was growing up, this was my favorite food. In fact, it still is. Would you like another piece, Missi?"

"Oh, yes! I think it's delicious."

During the rest of the dinner the conversation revolved around some of Maria's favorite Indian dishes and the upcoming arts-and-crafts fair. The tension slowly vanished as if someone had deflated a tire with a small puncture. The taut lines in Sloan's face relaxed into a half-grin as Missi began to respond to questions from Maria and Kendall.

"You made these plates!" Missi exclaimed to Maria when Kendall told the girl about her grandmother's skill.

"And every other container in this house," Kendall said with a laugh. "Grandma has a shed out back where she works, but this year she refuses to enter the fair. She claims that the folks around here get tired of seeing her pottery."

"These dishes are beautiful. I would never get tired of looking at them," Missi murmured as she ran a finger over the earthenware with a brown and blue geometric pattern.

"Would you like to see my workshop after dinner,

Missi?'' Maria asked as she stood and began to clear off the table.

"Can we stay, Daddy?'' Missi turned an excited face to her father.

"Sure. Kendall and I will do the dishes while you see the workshop.''

"You're a guest . . .''

Sloan's intense gaze snared Kendall's as he interrupted Maria's objection. "That's the least I can do for this delicious dinner you made for us.''

With Sloan's and her eyes still bound, Kendall hardly noticed Maria and Missi leaving the kitchen. Kendall's heartbeat was pounding, a weak ribbon running wildly through her and rendering her legs useless. Sloan's regard was lit with male interest as it leisurely traveled over her.

"Finally we are alone. I thought they would never leave.'' There was a playful note in his voice as the lazy glint in his midnight-dark eyes ignited a heated response within her betraying body.

"The shed is only ten yards out the back door.'' Her breathless answer barely carried across the table to him.

Sloan captured her hand and held it, his intent look singeing her. "Then I will have to work fast.''

"Fast?''

His grin spread, the lazy glint quickly developing into a bold appraisal of her fevered face. "I was hoping you would go fishing with Missi and me this weekend.''

Before she realized his intention, he had risen and was pulling her to her feet, his arms entwining about her and bringing her dangerously close to him. He had to know she wouldn't be able to refuse his invitation while in his embrace.

"I don't think . . ."

Sloan hushed her words with a light kiss on her lips. "I don't like the beginning of that answer. Try again, starting with the word 'yes,' followed by 'I would love to join you two.'"

"But Sloan, this is your time with Missi," Kendall protested weakly.

"I grant you it is, but at the same time she must realize that Sandra and I won't be getting back together."

Kendall tensed. "Don't use me to prove a point to Missi." She tried to pull free of his embrace, but his arms became a band of steel about her.

All playfulness evaporated from the atmosphere to be replaced with a razor-sharp tension that vibrated between them as Sloan stared down at Kendall. "That was unfair, Kendall, and you know it. A divorce is rough on any child, but Missi has an added problem—her asthma. Sandra and I never have seen eye to eye on Missi's asthma. Sandra wants to wrap Missi up in a protective cocoon and shield her from the rest of the world. I want Missi to know her limitations, then do as much as she can. She thinks she's abnormal and that has led to some difficult problems." Sloan released his hold on Kendall as he spoke and stepped a few feet away.

"Sloan, have you thought about letting Missi learn to swim? Swimming doesn't have the effect other physical activities have on someone with asthma. Chris has been doing great and he feels like he's normal, participating in a sport like the other kids."

"Until this last week I rarely had a say in raising my daughter. Sandra would ignore everything I said about Missi, and since I worked long hours on my project, there was little I could do about it. I saw things happening and yet my hands were tied where Missi was concerned." Turning on his heel, he leaned into the sink and stared out the window over it. "Dammit, Kendall, I feel so guilty. I feel like I let my daughter down with the divorce and everything. But strangely, with my visitation rights, I have more say over Missi now than before. I don't have to fight with Sandra every step of the way now when I want to do something with my own child."

Kendall laid a hand on his shoulder, kneading the tight muscles beneath her fingers. "I've seen parents argue before over a child who has a chronic illness. It's not easy on anyone concerned. You can do only what you think is right."

Sloan stilled the motion of her hand and turned to face Kendall, his fingers closing around hers. He lifted his other hand and cupped her face, studying her in tender silence. The warm glow in his eyes accelerated her pulse to a wild pace as he stroked her cheek with infinite gentleness.

"Of course, I know logically there's no reason to berate myself over past mistakes. All you can do is learn from them. But things aren't always logical, Kendall."

How well she was finding that out with Sloan, Kendall thought. There was nothing logical about her intense attraction to him!

"But Missi and I have made a start and I plan on talking with Sandra again," Sloan continued. "Somehow I have to convince her to let Missi go a little. For the next month Missi will have swimming lessons. That much I can do. Then maybe Sandra will continue them when she returns to Atlanta.''

Both of his hands were framing her face now and Kendall was mesmerized by them, held immobile by his drugging touches, his adoring eyes. She struggled to say something, to end the spellbound trance, but her voice was stolen by the impact of her flaming desire and by the power of his.

Slowly, leisurely, he closed the distance between their mouths, her face still within his hands. As his lips tenderly, softly sampled hers, slanting tentatively across them, she had no desire to stop the magic he was encasing her in. It felt wonderful, blissful, especially when he coaxed her lips apart and his tongue slipped into her mouth, tasting and exploring, dueling with hers in a sweet battle.

Kendall's arms went about Sloan as he fitted her slenderness against his sinewy hardness. His hands drifted from her face to her shoulders, then down to her hips, where they rested, molding her to him, making her vividly aware of the effect she had on him.

''You're a special woman, Kendall Spencer,'' he whispered against her before again taking her lips in a fierce claim, parting them and plunging into the dark recesses of her mouth.

When he removed his lips from hers and began to kiss her ear, she felt as if every nerve were on fire, as if every muscle and bone were being consumed by a raging inferno. Her hands roamed restlessly over his back, achingly wanting to feel his bare skin beneath them instead of the material of his shirt.

"You care, Kendall," he murmured between tiny nips on her earlobe that sent a tremor of excitement through her. Lifting his head away from her, he stared down into her passionate gaze, continuing in a voice laden with his own desire. "You helped Missi through a difficult time today and I can't thank you enough for that." A crooked half-smile crept into his features as he added, "And don't tell me you were only doing your job. Lady, I can feel how much you care. I can see it. It goes beyond being a doctor."

Kendall's arms tightened around Sloan, her eyes misting at the depth of his feeling. She indeed felt very special in that moment under his intensely absorbing look. His appearance in her life struck a primitive chord within her that she hadn't known existed. When he looked at her as he was doing at the moment, she felt as though she were drowning in the pure sensuality of the man.

Sloan pulled her close to him and held her in a vehement embrace that threatened her next breath. "Thank you, Kendall, for being there for Missi."

Kendall swallowed hard, reluctantly placing a few inches between them as she said in a voice that quavered slightly, "Grandma and Missi are going to wonder what we have been doing if we don't get these dishes done." Stepping away, she desperately fought the sense of losing control. Sloan's opinion was becoming very important to her and she was scared of what might happen when he left next month, when he was no longer around to give her that opinion. The thought of growing dependent on his friendship, his presence in her life, then to have it withdrawn, chilled her.

"I don't think we could fool your grandmother for one second."

Sloan's deep voice swiftly took her away from her thoughts. At the moment it was easier not to think.

"She's a very sharp lady. Must run in the family," Sloan added with a rakish grin.

Kendall actually blushed again for the second time in years. "All these compliments will go to my head if you don't stop, Sloan Hunter." She tilted her head to one side and studied him for a brief moment. "Are you trying to get me to do all the work, sir? If so, it won't work. I'll wash. You dry."

He arched a brow. "You don't have a dishwasher?"

"Yes. Me."

Quickly Kendall began clearing off the table and stacking the dishes before she succumbed to her keen impulse to bring his lips down onto hers and delve her tongue into his mouth. Her lips still tingled from the recent pressure of his; her pulse still raced from the memory of his hands on her, pressing her into him.

At the sink she squirted some liquid soap into the water and watched the bubbles form, as though they were the most fascinating things to see. In reality she knew he was observing her and she didn't want him to see her confusion, her conflicting emotions that continually surfaced at the oddest times.

"I'll pick you up at five tomorrow morning." His warm breath tickled her ear as he kissed her neck.

She twisted about and exclaimed, "Five!" The lingering impression of his light kiss burned into her.

"Remember our fishing expedition?"

"Oh," was all she could think of to say.

Sloan reached around her, his arm brushing hers, as he turned off the water. A teasing gleam sparkled in his eyes as they engaged hers. "We would have had a hard time explaining that," he said, indicating the sink full of water.

While Kendall started washing the dishes, Sloan searched the kitchen for a towel. "There's one in that drawer by the stove," Kendall said as she placed the first plate in the drain. "Are you sure, Sloan?"

"Sure?" He straightened, pushed the drawer closed with his knee and turned around to look at her. "About your going?"

She nodded.

"It's been a long time since I've been this sure about something." He crossed the room in three strides and picked up the plate to dry. "Besides, who else would show us the best place to fish on Crystal Lake?" A devil winked at her while an angel flashed a smile.

"I don't know if I should give out the local secrets. Give me one good reason why I should."

He seized her wet hand and hauled her between him and the counter in a quick tug. The angelical smile was gone but the devil was still there. "Because I'm such a nice guy and desperate to show my daughter that I know how to fish. So far, I've caught one fish that had to be thrown back in because it was too small. Now, would you want my failing in the eyes of my daughter on your conscience?''

Silent laughter exploded in his dark eyes while his thumb rubbed sensual circles at her wrist, making it near impossible to think of a comeback. Instead, Kendall murmured, ''No.''

His head lowered slowly toward hers, as if he were giving her a chance to pull back if she wanted to. But she was lost in the swirling depths of his eyes, in his utterly male appeal. His arms encircled her, his lips seeking the warmth of hers. The kiss began gently, then quickly evolved into a savage mating with them clinging together as if each were the other's life raft.

They parted when they heard voices outside the screen door and Sloan chuckled softly as he turned his undivided attention to drying the dishes. ''I feel like a teen-ager caught in the act of kissing my girl by her parents.''

Kendall didn't make a comment, but when he had said ''my girl,'' her heart missed a beat. She couldn't help but wonder what it would be like if they lived in the same town and had a chance to really get to know each other.

''Daddy, Maria said she would teach me how to make a bowl if it's all right with you. Can I? Please.'' Missi stood next to Maria, the little girl's face alive with enthusiasm.

''I don't see why not, if you're sure.''

''I enjoy teaching.'' Maria eyed the still-dirty dishes, her eyes twinkling with barely suppressed curiosity.

''I can vouch for that. I was her pupil once, Missi.''

Kendall hoped her face didn't look as flushed as she felt it did.

"Can we start tomorrow? I want to enter my bowl in the fair," Missi said eagerly.

"It will have to be tomorrow afternoon. We're going fishing in the morning. Kendall is coming with us."

Holding her breath, Kendall waited for Missi's response to Sloan's announcement. For a few seconds the atmosphere thickened.

"That will be perfect. I have to meet with Flora in the morning and won't be free until after three. Why don't you come to the workshop at four?" Maria cut into the heavy silence.

Missi looked up at her father and he nodded.

"Fine. Now, you all leave my kitchen and let me finish cleaning up," Maria commanded, scooting them away with a wave of her hands.

"If we're going to be up before dawn, then we'd better be going, Missi," Sloan said.

As they were walking toward the front door, Kendall stopped, snapping her fingers. "I haven't called Chris yet. I'll only be a minute."

Kendall quickly turned toward the den and made a call to Chris while Missi and Sloan waited on the front porch. She set a date with Chris to come over to the house the next afternoon after Missi's pottery lesson.

At the news, Missi seemed to float out to Sloan's car a few minutes later. The next day was going to be a big one for her and she didn't even object to Sloan's telling her she had to get to bed early, which brought a stunned look to his face.

"Just as I think I have my child all figured out, she goes and surprises me. I think being a parent is the hardest job there is," Sloan said with a low chuckle as Missi slid into the car.

"Children keep you on your toes," Kendall said, intending to step away to allow him to leave. But the shattering look he gave her stopped her. In the light from the porch she saw clearly the desire for her in his eyes. It matched the look in hers.

He leaned closer and whispered, "We have to stop meeting like this."

"Like what?"

"With everybody in the world around us."

His lips grazed hers briefly, the touch fleeting but searing her with his passion, with his intentions. The last of her defenses crumbled into dust.

Chapter Six

*H*ere. It looks like you could use a cup of coffee.''
Sloan finished pouring the hot brew from a Thermos,
then handed Kendall the red plastic cup.

The coffee was accompanied with a warm smile and
Kendall appreciated both. She hadn't slept well again the
night before and she could barely keep her eyes open.
After taking a few sips, Kendall finally said, ''I must
have been crazy to agree to this ungodly hour.''

Sloan glanced amusedly at her before starting the
engine. ''I thought all fishermen got up at this hour.
Since I haven't had much luck late in the day, mid-
morning, or during the afternoon, I thought I would try
this time. Now, where to?''

''Go to the end of this street, take a left and head for
the far side of the lake.'' Kendall drank another sip of
coffee, then twisted about and smiled at Missi, who sat

in the backseat, which was really not a backseat but a storage area big enough for a child to sit in. "Good morning. At least I think it is. It's hard to tell when the sun isn't even up yet."

Kendall's stomach muscles tensed as she waited for Missi's response. One of the reasons she had had trouble sleeping the previous night had been Missi. Would the morning be one long battle with Sloan's daughter?

But Missi giggled. "You should have seen Daddy this morning trying to fix the coffee."

Missi's excitement was quickly spreading throughout the car as Sloan quipped, "Yeah, Doc. I need you to look at my shin. I think I broke it stumbling into a chair that a certain young lady I know left pulled out last night." He peered over his shoulder at Missi as they waited at a stop sign. "Do you often set traps for your poor, unsuspecting father?"

"Oh, Daddy!"

By the time they reached the place that Kendall had decided would be the best spot to fish at this time of year, the sky had lightened to a pinkish gray and they were all laughing at Sloan's description of getting ready for the fishing expedition.

"And if that wasn't enough, I locked the cabin door with the keys to the car still inside. Thank God a window was unlocked or I would have had to resort to desperate means." Sloan climbed from the car and went around to open the hatchback.

"Sounds like you're a night person," Kendall teased as she rounded the car to help unload it.

"Definitely. I think I was the crazy one to suggest this

hour. See how far a father will go to impress his daughter? I just hope you appreciate this sacrifice, Missi.''

Missi beamed under her father's kidding while he handed her the three fishing poles.

''Ah, a blanket. Just what I need to stretch out on and sleep.'' Kendall took the blanket and a knapsack from the back, and headed for the edge of the lake with Missi. ''After all, I've done my share. I've shown you the secret fishing hole,'' she tossed over her shoulder.

''Only time will tell that,'' Sloan called out, his arms laden with the rest of the fishing equipment and a cooler filled with ice.

After placing the blanket and knapsack on the ground, Kendall straightened, her attention drawn to the flaming horizon, where the sun was rising, tinting the gray darkness with its bright illumination.

''Mmm. Isn't that beautiful?'' Kendall murmured in the early morning quiet to Missi, who stopped next to her, still holding the fishing rods. ''I suppose it's worth getting up to see the beauty of a sunrise, especially over the lake.''

They stood side by side gazing at the sunrise for a long moment, the tranquil silence broken occasionally by a bird or the soft rustle of the leaves in the light breeze. Sloan came up behind Missi and Kendall to join them, laying his hands on Missi's shoulders. It was a time of sharing, a time of forgetting everything but the present.

''I'm afraid, ladies, if we don't get going, the fish will all go back to sleep.'' Sloan playfully slapped both of them on the bottom. ''Okay, rule number one: each of us baits his own fishing pole. And rule number two, the most important one: no one—I repeat, no one—out-fishes the leader of this expedition.''

A smile pulled up the corners of Kendall's mouth. ''I wonder who the leader is, Missi. Do you have any idea?''

Joining in on the fun, Missi exaggerated a shrug. ''Nope.''

''Me!'' Sloan pointed to himself. ''And don't you two ladies forget it. Just remember, I have the keys to the car.'' He dangled the keys in front of them before pocketing them. ''It's a long walk back,'' he said in mock seriousness, but his eyes gleamed with suppressed laughter; his mouth twitched from trying to contain his amusement.

''Daddy! You wouldn't make us walk.''

Sloan folded his arms across his chest and looked up toward the trees as though he were giving the whole situation careful consideration. ''I might be persuaded to reconsider, but the safest course of action is to follow the rules.''

''Missi, is your father always this underhanded?'' Kendall asked, warm laughter in her question.

''Of course I am. How else would I always get my way? Missi, give Kendall her fishing pole and let's hop to it. What we catch is what we have for lunch. And nothing, my fair ladies, wouldn't satisfy my huge appetite.''

Kendall balled her hands and placed them on her hips. ''Make up your mind, Sloan Hunter. Either we catch fish or we don't.''

His laughter rang deep in the stillness. "I never said don't catch fish. Just don't catch one bigger than mine."

The light, bantering mood became infectious as the three sat patiently on the bank with their poles in the water. Occasionally Missi would retreat from the conversation, but each time Sloan determinedly drew her back in, making her aware that she was an equal partner in whatever they were discussing. At those times, Kendall could see Missi warring with herself. The girl still saw Kendall as a threat for her father's affection, and yet Missi's initial hostility was gone. Kendall suspected her handling of Missi's asthma episode in her office the day before had helped deflate some of Missi's anger toward her.

An hour passed, the sun rose above the trees, but the cooler where the fish were to be kept remained empty.

"I think the fish went back to sleep, Daddy."

"Patience, hon. That's part of fishing." But Sloan shifted on the bank as if he were about to pull in his fishing rod for the day.

"Well, I'm hungry. Did you bring breakfast or were we to eat fish for breakfast, too?" Kendall asked, peering sideways toward Sloan.

"I'm a very thorough leader. Of course I brought breakfast for us. I'm offended you could even think otherwise." Sloan frowned but winked at Missi, mischief lurking in his dark brown eyes. "In the knapsack. And for doubting my wonderful leadership, you can fix it."

"Three breakfasts coming up." Kendall reeled in her

line, then hopped to her feet, brushing off her jeans before heading up the slope to the blanket.

Kendall prepared their "breakfast" of doughnuts and orange juice while Missi and Sloan continued to fish. Looking up once, Kendall discovered Sloan staring at her, all mischief gone and in its place a message of desire, silently directed straight at her. Even though the morning was already growing warm, his intent regard sent chills of arousal coursing through her as if his hands were exploring her flesh inch by delicious inch.

Missi's squeals of delight pierced Kendall's sensual haze, and she swung her attention toward the nine-year-old, calming her spinning senses with a deep breath.

"Daddy! Daddy, I got a fish! And it's huge!"

"Reel it in carefully, hon. That's our lunch."

Kendall took pleasure in watching Sloan and Missi while the girl reeled in the fish. He moved with a coordinated, wiry toughness that gave an impression of leashed energy, held barely in restraint. As he spoke to Missi, his voice was rough and warm at the same time with a gritty huskiness that reflected the undeniable maleness in him.

When Sloan twisted about, raising his arm to display to Kendall the big trout Missi had caught, his broad smile froze on his lips as their gazes met and silently imparted their needs across the expanse. It was a brief, charged moment in which Kendall was only aware of his lean, sardonic features and his penetrating dark eyes, which reached into her soul and read what was there. The moment fled as quickly as it came, and Kendall looked down at the breakfast she had prepared for them.

"It's going to be hard to beat that fish, Missi." Thank goodness her voice worked. She didn't think her legs would, though. "Breakfast is ready, you two. Let's celebrate." Her voice grew stronger, steadier, as she kept her eyes diverted from Sloan's.

But when Missi and he sat across from her on the blanket, Kendall felt his perceptive eyes boring into her, demanding she look up at him. Her willpower was all but gone as she lifted her eyelids and centered her complete attention upon the man across from her. A shudder rippled through her entire body as she catalogued each of his features, etched in desire.

Severing their visual contact, Sloan said, "I've got my work cut out for me. You sure could have caught a smaller fish, Missi. What are you trying to do, put your dad to shame?"

Missi's smile was wide, encompassing her whole face.

"At least you'll have something for lunch, thanks to Missi," Kendall said, feeling a sense of family as they sat on the blanket eating their doughnuts.

After breakfast they all perched on the bank again and fished. Kendall caught two small catfish while Missi brought in another trout. But by eleven o'clock Sloan still hadn't reeled in one fish!

"Do you give up, Sloan Hunter, and admit your daughter is a better fisherman—or is that fisherwoman?"

"I never admit defeat. We'll just have to come back another day. I didn't want to show you two up the first day."

Missi and Kendall looked at each other, then burst out laughing.

"The arrogance of the male species." Kendall rolled her eyes heavenward as she shook her head slowly in disbelief.

Sloan's eyes widened, a mocking glint dancing in their depths. "Is this mutiny in the ranks?"

"You bet!" Kendall retorted with a laugh, bringing in her fishing line and standing. "I don't know about you two, but I'm starved. Those doughnuts hardly satisfied me. If you expect me to work all morning, you have to feed me."

Sloan slowly reeled his line in, then rose, coming face to face with Kendall. "Woman, you have some appetite," he growled in a low voice for her ears only before turning to Missi and instructing her to bring in her line, too.

And Kendall was finding out she had some appetite, too: she wanted Sloan Hunter; she wanted his tanned fingers to caress her, to stroke her skin into a fiery readiness; she wanted to hear him whisper love words into her ear, then to touch her until a raging inferno sped through her bloodstream; she wanted to tremble with wild abandon, to give to him as she would take from him. In that instant as they prepared to leave, she discovered she wanted a lot—a relationship that wouldn't end when he went back to St. Louis.

Kendall hardly spoke during the drive to Sloan's cabin, where they were going to fry the trout. She contented herself with listening to Missi and Sloan talk about the morning activities and the pottery lesson later that day for Missi.

When they arrived at the cabin, Amy was out front, having just stepped off the front porch. Sloan brought the car to a stop and Missi was out the door in a flash. As Sloan and Kendall emptied the back of the car and carried the gear up to the porch, Missi was telling Amy all about their outing and the fish she caught.

"Daddy, can Amy eat with us?"

"If it's all right with her parents."

"We'll go ask," Missi called out, already having turned away.

Before Sloan could say he would call, the two girls were running toward the Frasers' cabin. A frown stretched tightly over his lips.

"What's wrong?" Kendall probed gently, her hand hovering near his shoulder for a few seconds before she touched him, his body warmth a lure she couldn't resist.

"Sandra always told me that Missi shouldn't run. Then there is always that damned dog. What if it's still around here and attacks one of them?"

"We can see the Frasers' cabin from here and keep an eye on the girls without their knowing it. That way Missi will feel she has some independence."

"And she hasn't had much of that." His frown deepened, contorting his features.

"It's hard not to want to protect your child from dangers. There are times, though, a parent has to stand back and let the child discover her limits."

A faint smile shone through the frown. "I think I told

you that was what I intended to do.'' Sloan's arm went about her and he hugged her to him. "It's about time that Missi has some freedom if she's ever going to grow up. Later this afternoon, I think I'll call about those swimming lessons. Let's go inside and fry those fish."

Kendall returned his smile. "Do you think we can manage?" she asked.

Both of his eyebrows rose. "Surely you were kidding about not knowing how to cook! With a grandmother who cooks such heavenly dishes, you had to absorb some of her knowledge."

Kendall shook her head.

"Not even this much?" Sloan indicated an inch with his forefinger and thumb.

"Sorry."

"Maybe the Frasers would like to join us for lunch, too, and fix the lunch while they're here." He grinned, deviltry in his expression.

Kendall slipped her arm about his waist. "We'll manage. I can read a cookbook. Surely we can figure out what to do. We are two reasonably intelligent people."

Grabbing the handle of the cooler while Kendall opened the door, Sloan asked, "How did things ever get to this sad state?"

"I have a feeling we were both too busy to learn a mundane chore like cooking."

"Don't let Julia Child hear you say that."

Inside the small kitchen it was hard to concentrate on reading the old cookbook that Sloan had found in a drawer, left behind by his colleague, who owned the cabin. Sloan's nearness was too distracting for Kendall as she bent over the book that sat on the countertop and studied the different recipes for preparing fish.

Sloan came up behind her and whispered into her ear, "Don't get fancy on me." His hand touched hers as he pointed to a recipe for frying fish, the contact scorching her arm. "This one looks simple enough. Let's see, we just fry the fish at three hundred seventy-five degrees for three to five minutes on both sides. Doesn't sound like there's anything to it."

When he pulled his hand back and brushed her again, a sudden rush of fire suffused her whole body at his mere touch. Marshaling all her failing self-control, she stepped away from him before she dissolved.

"Sometimes the simplest things are the hardest. I'll reserve my judgment until I'm sitting at the table eating the fish."

He pinned her with a piercing, knowing look. "Kendall, you have to have more faith that things will somehow manage to work out."

The double meaning wasn't lost on her. She had always been such a rational realist that it was difficult to think their situation would work out for the best in the end. If she allowed her life to be placed in fate's hands and let her emotions rule her future, she would end up being hurt by Sloan. But still it was hard to ignore her clamoring senses that screamed their need for his total possession. She wasn't a superwoman!

She smiled deliberately and said in a forced lightness, "If we're ever going to eat those fish, we'd better start frying them. You fry. I'll make a salad. I can at least do that.''

Standing at the counter, Kendall concentrated on tearing the lettuce into small bits, trying her best not to look at Sloan, who was whistling a merry tune.

She had placed the salad on the table when Sloan returned from checking on the girls, who were playing out front. When he entered the kitchen, their gazes immediately sought each other. Sloan shortened the distance between them in two long strides. His hand came up to smooth a strand of hair away from her face as he regarded her with a leisurely thoroughness.

"How are the girls?" Kendall asked, her voice wavering.

"Fine."

His hands clasped her shoulders, and with a tug, he flattened her against him. His mouth opened over hers, urging her lips apart to investigate her hidden recesses in tender slowness. She felt the tremor in his hands as he lengthened the kiss, their mouths mating in a soul-searching union.

His hands slid down her length to anchor her more firmly to him as he buried his face in her hair. "I want to know everything there is to know about you, Kendall. I would never hurt you, darling," he murmured.

Kendall wedged a small space between them and touched his beard-roughened jaw. For a brief moment her attention focused fully on the contrast of his jaw to the smoothness of his lips as she traced their outline. She felt, as well as saw, those lips lift upward in a beguiling smile.

"Didn't have time to shave this morning, Doc," he explained.

"Sloan, I believe you wouldn't knowingly hurt me, but sometimes it just happens. I've been through one bad experience and I don't know if I'm ready for another one."

His features tensed into a frown. "I see. You've decided it's a foregone conclusion that I'll hurt you. Thanks, Kendall, for the vote of confidence."

She met his anger with an unshakable directness, the disturbing impact of his stare slicing into her with a shrewd sharpness. He disengaged himself from her and moved away. The seconds stretched into an uncomfortable minute as her thoughts raced wildly in an attempt to find the right words to explain her confusion.

"I don't think you do see, Sloan. You live in St. Louis and I live here."

"I don't need a geography lesson, Kendall." He ran his hand repeatedly through his hair, his gaze drilling into her in an unbearably intense appraisal. Then abruptly he looked away and crossed the room to the stove, where he flipped over the fish.

The grim set of his shoulders and the rigid line of his back underscored his anger and frustration. What Kendall had said was right, logically speaking, but what he was feeling for her wasn't logical.

Finally he twisted about. "You're right, Kendall, but I'm not going to leave you alone. I still want to get to know you, and when I set my mind to do something, it's hard to divert me." He advanced toward her, the tautness draining away, his tone softening. "There is something between us and you can't deny it. All the logic in the world can't change the fact that we are definitely attracted to each other."

Kendall was becoming weak from the power of his regard. "But, Sloan . . ."

Quickly, his hand grazed her cheek. All words were lost in the mayhem his touch produced in Kendall. His tantalizing closeness was her undoing. She fell into his embrace and relished his strength that enveloped her.

"Don't you see, if we become involved, Sloan, and fall in love, you'll expect me to give up my practice in Spencerville and move to St. Louis. I can't. I won't do that."

"You don't know that I would ask that of you."

"It's only normal that you would. The woman is expected to give up her job for the man."

"I'm not like most men, Kendall. You can't plan and map out the course of a relationship. Too many unexpected things can occur," he whispered against her hair, his hands roaming up and down her back, molding her closer to him. "I want you in every sense of the word, but you'll call the shots."

The fervor in his voice told Kendall he wanted her and she nestled against him, glorying in the feel of being desired.

Something burning broke them apart and Sloan rushed to the stove to remove the frying fish. One side of the trout was slightly charred. They looked at each other, a smile flirting at the corners of Sloan's mouth.

His smile grew into a gust of laughter as he stared at her as she tried to contain her amusement. "Don't you dare say it!"

"I'd never say I told you so." Innocence bathed Kendall's face.

"Oh, no, never," he grumbled good-naturedly. "You might as well tell the girls lunch is ready."

As Kendall was about to leave the kitchen, Sloan captured her wrist, bringing her back around to face him. "Kendall, I haven't ignored the fact that we live in different places, but I've always made it a policy not to worry about a problem until it becomes a problem." He smiled, trying to inject some humor into the situation. "It's easier on my stomach that way."

She tried to match his smile, but her mouth wouldn't cooperate. "I'll try to follow your advice, but I'm not made that way. I worry. I do plan for the future."

"I've been hurt, too, but if you aren't willing to take chances, you'll never be truly happy. Yes, you and I getting to know each other, becoming friends—lovers— will be taking a chance. I'm willing to take the risk. Are you?"

"Yes—no. I don't know! What do you want me to say? I've known you only a week."

"Nothing right now. I told you I would give you time, and I will."

"But we don't have the time! That's the problem." Kendall felt as if the walls were closing in on her, that time had become her enemy.

"St. Louis isn't the end of the world, Kendall. I own a

plane and love to fly. That cuts the distance in time between here and St. Louis at least in half.''

"You're a pilot?" Part of her grasped on to that fact, her hope blossoming.

"The only reason I didn't fly down for this vacation was because I wanted the use of my car while I was here. You see, we can work things out if we both want it badly enough and try hard enough.''

In that moment Kendall believed they could. She wanted to believe they could. She moved closer and started to speak when Missi and Amy came bounding into the cabin, starved and ready to devour the slightly burned fish.

"I've never been in a small plane before," Kendall said, sitting down on the porch swing at her house, Sloan lounging next to her with his arm stretched out along the back of it.

"Well, I'll just have to remedy that. Sometime I'll fly my plane down and take you for a ride.''

The implication of his words brought a smile to her lips. She liked the thought that they had a future together. She pushed her own doubts to the back of her mind and instead leaned back, Sloan's arm dropping about her shoulders, gently caressing her upper arm.

Taking a sip of her iced tea, Kendall said, "I enjoyed myself this morning and I think Missi did, too.''

"She's coming around. She's really a very sweet child, if I do say so myself. I just have to keep remembering that when she is complaining that she hasn't seen me since Christmas." A frown flickered over his features. "Christmas last year wasn't a fun holiday. She spent the whole time crying and trying to convince me that Sandra wasn't happy with Ted. By the time she had left I felt about an inch tall."

Kendall could feel his frustration that the memory of Christmas had conjured up. She twisted her head to look up into his eyes. Her skin pricked with fiery awareness as his raking gaze missed nothing—not the look of compassion in her eyes, not her slightly parted lips that yearned for the feel of his on hers, nor the tenseness that had entered her features, sharpening her senses to his every movement.

The silence stretched between them as Kendall silently gave him her support. He touched her cheek with the back of his hand, stroking her with a tenderness she hadn't thought possible from a man a week before. Taking her glass from her, he released her gaze, placing the tea on the table, then pulling her close to him.

"Do you want to talk about it, Sloan? I know children have a way of playing on our guilt."

Kendall sat next to him, her head on his shoulder as he rambled on. Since the breakup of his marriage, he had kept everything bottled up inside of him. Yes, he felt guilty about Missi, but at the same time he knew that to stay married to Sandra would have been worse on his daughter in the long run. Kendall's gentle voice, her compassion, disarmed his usual defenses and he found himself telling her about Sandra and Missi.

He concluded by saying, "Sandra and I were high-school sweethearts. Looking back now, I can see where we went wrong. We married at eighteen, fresh out of high school. I had a trust fund that paid for my college education, but it was still a struggle to make ends meet. That should have brought us closer together, but it didn't. Through the years we grew apart, our interests going in opposite directions. I wanted different things out of life than she.''

"The end to any relationship is hard even if there is no love between the two people involved.''

"Were you two planning to marry?''

Her soft gray eyes mirrored the hurt she had had to deal with when Blake had ended their relationship; she found his question disturbing. Slowly, after a long pause, she answered, "I thought so, but I don't think he did.'' Until Sloan had asked that question, she hadn't faced that fact. But she could see that she had read more into their relationship than there had been. She wouldn't allow herself to take anything for granted again.

"Hi, Dr. Spencer,'' a young boy called from the yard, laying his bike on the grass and mounting the porch steps.

"Hello, Chris. I want you to meet Missi's father, Dr. Hunter.''

The young boy held his hand out and shook Sloan's. "It's nice to meet you, sir,'' Chris replied in a shy, quiet voice.

"Missi should be through in a few minutes. Would you like something to drink, Chris?'' Kendall asked, gesturing for the ten-year-old to be seated in one of the white wicker chairs.

"A Coke, if you have one.''

Kendall left Chris and Sloan to talk while she fixed the boy a drink. She needed a moment away from Sloan to collect her thoughts. While he had spoken about his divorce and about the difficulties he was having with Missi, she had sensed that he didn't talk much about his problems to anyone, that she had been the first one. She was pleased he had confided in her, but at the same time it placed a responsibility on her. She had realized as he had talked about his past that she never wanted to be responsible for causing the pain that was reflected in his voice, his eyes. If she encouraged his friendship and a relationship between them, she had to be prepared to make it work even after his vacation was over. But could a long-distance relationship bring fulfillment for both of them? That question, unanswered, disturbed her the whole time she stalled going back out onto the porch.

Finally she heard Missi and her grandmother talking with Chris and Sloan and knew she had to return with Chris's Coke. Slowly she made her way to the front porch, greeting everyone with a smile that was an effort to keep in place.

Missi was bubbling with excitement, quickly wiping away any tension that Kendall felt as the girl explained what she had done. As Missi told Sloan about the bowl she was making, Kendall's gaze rested on his handsome features, her full attention homing in on his lips, which could be hard and demanding, unrelenting, stubborn, or gentle, working like an erotic drug on her senses.

She shifted her attention to his eyes, a dark brown, almost black, with an expressive, disquieting depth to them. Suddenly his gaze moved, trapping hers with an amused, knowing regard. Missi had finished explaining about her first pottery lesson and was talking with Chris about his swimming. But to Kendall Missi's words flowed over her with no meaning, as all of Kendall's senses became centered on Sloan, the raw impact of his gaze doing strange things to her insides.

Slowly, hesitantly, Kendall realized where she was and reluctantly looked away from Sloan, trying to assemble her scattered poise, but not before she saw the incredibly gentle smile in Sloan's eyes.

"Daddy is letting me take swimming lessons, Chris. My first one is at six today." Missi tilted her chin at a proud angle.

"I'm going to the pool right now to practice for a swim meet this weekend. The meet is here in Spencerville. Would you like to come Saturday morning and see me swim?" Chris asked, his initial shyness at meeting a new person gone in his own enthusiasm.

"Can we, Daddy?"

"Sure," Sloan replied, glancing down at his watch. "In fact, if we don't get a move on it, you're going to be late for your first lesson. Would you like a ride, Chris?"

"No, thanks. I have my bike." Chris turned to leave, saying to Missi, "See you later at the pool."

"Gosh, he's lucky. He even gets to ride a bike," Missi said when Chris had pedaled away.

Sloan tensed, but said in a smooth, controlled voice, "You'd better get your swimming suit, hon."

"You left it in the workshop," Kendall's grandmother said. "Let's go through the house, Missi, and get a few of those cookies I promised you."

When Missi and Maria left, Kendall sat down on the swing again. A subtle tension hung in the air. Kendall sensed that where Missi was concerned, Sloan felt very helpless at times, especially since he didn't have her most of the year. Being a vacation father was taking its toll on him.

"Will you come with us to the pool?" Sloan asked in a quiet voice, leaning forward, his elbows on his knees, his hands dangling between his long legs.

She wanted to reach out and touch him, but for some reason she felt he had retreated behind a wall. Perhaps he felt exposed, uncomfortable because she had glimpsed his vulnerability.

"Sloan, I think you two should go alone."

"Why? I wanted this to be a day the three of us spent together."

"Like a family?" Kendall asked bluntly.

"Yes."

"It's my turn to ask why."

Sloan twisted his head to spear her with a keen look. Slowly, he answered, "I'm not sure, Kendall. I think because I'm basically a family man. The single life holds no attraction for me."

Her throat constricted. She sensed it had been hard for him to admit that. "I'll go. In fact, I think I'll swim some laps." *To work off some of my frustration*, she silently added.

* * *

Kendall finished her thirty laps and hauled herself out of the water, exhausted but strangely relaxed. Sloan was talking with Missi's swimming teacher. Having completed the arrangements for Missi's extra lessons, some of them private, Sloan turned toward Kendall and smiled.

"Ready to go?" he asked.

Kendall nodded. "I don't think any of us will have trouble sleeping tonight."

Kendall noticed Missi's excitement had ebbed in the past fifteen minutes as the day's activities finally caught up with her. On the ride back to Kendall's house, Missi fell asleep in the cramped backseat.

"You know what she told me," Sloan said, gesturing toward his daughter. "That not one of those kids in the class knew she had asthma. Until she had said that to me, I hadn't realized it, but Sandra had always made it known about Missi's asthma—not only to her teachers, but to her playmates and their parents as well." Sloan's jaw knotted. At a stoplight, he braced a palm against the steering wheel, turning to look across at Kendall. "I get the feeling that today is the first time my daughter has felt normal in a long time." For a few seconds he shifted his glance toward Missi, then back to Kendall, his brow knitted. "What can I do about it? Look at Chris. He seems to be coping quite well."

"You made a good start today, Sloan. She really enjoyed the swimming lesson. Talk with Sandra. Tell her about the lessons and how well Missi did."

The crease in his brow strengthened into a scowl. "That won't be easy. But what I do for the short time I have Missi won't mean much if Sandra continues to cloister her."

At her house, Kendall started to get out of the car when Sloan seized her wrist and prevented her from leaving. "This time I'll walk you to the door."

A deliciously wicked glint in his eyes immobilized her. Today he had confided in her and she felt privileged to be in his confidence. He had trusted her with his innermost thoughts and that thrilled her.

He released her wrist and climbed from the car, rounding the front to open her door. The whole time she watched him move, reveling in the sight of him. She was storing these moments for when he would have to return to St. Louis and her life would have to proceed without him. Her heartbeat slowed at that thought.

Sloan held his hand out and she slipped hers into his strong grasp, his fingers fitting wonderfully around hers like a secure, warm sheath. They walked across the lawn and mounted the steps to the front porch in silence.

At the door Kendall turned in toward Sloan, staring up into his eyes for an endless moment. She wanted to ask when she would see him again, but she remained quiet. She didn't have a right to ask.

As though he had read her thoughts, he said, "I'll call you tomorrow. You know you have to give me a chance to beat you at fishing."

"I don't know why. I like it the way it stands now," she quipped mischievously.

"And dent my male pride!" Sloan exclaimed in feigned amazement.

"I don't think I have to worry about that. You seem pretty strong to me."

"We all have our weak points, Kendall." A serious note edged his voice.

All humor vanished. Suddenly exposed raw emotions stood between them as Sloan's arms folded her tightly, tenderly against him. "What is it about you that makes me want to pour out my soul to you? Are you a witch? I've never talked so much about myself, and certainly not in one day," he whispered against the top of her head, then pulled slightly away to stare down at her in astonishment. "And I still don't know much about you."

She attempted a smile, but her eyes remained a cool silver. All of a sudden she wanted to retreat from the conversation. "There isn't much to know."

"I disagree. You've been terribly hurt in the past and that makes you afraid to open up to a man. Trust me, Kendall."

"I'm trying, Sloan. It's just not easy."

"Okay, darling. I'm all patience."

Sloan bent forward and kissed her, deeply, passionately, and with infinite tenderness, spreading a warm glow throughout her body. She wanted to prolong the kiss, but Sloan severed it, placing her at arm's length.

"If I don't go now, Missi might spend the night in the backseat of the car."

A bright smile camouflaged the disappointment Kendall had felt when he pulled away. "Good night, Sloan."

Sloan waited until Kendall was inside the house before heading back to his car. The long, silent drive to the cabin afforded him an opportunity to think. Each time he went over the developing relationship between himself and Kendall, his determination to get to know the real Kendall Spencer was cemented more firmly in his mind.

After parking his car in front of the cabin, he carried Missi inside. Sleepily she got ready for bed without a protest to the early hour. Sloan kissed Missi good-night, then left her bedroom to fix himself a drink and relax on the porch. This time of evening, as the sun was setting, was his favorite time of day. It provoked in his mind thoughts of him and Kendall that evening at the cove. But tonight he had to decide what to do about talking with Sandra.

He had finished pouring some whiskey into a glass when the phone rang. "Hello, Hunter speaking."

"This is Sandra, Sloan. May I speak with Missi?"

Every muscle in his body tensed; his hold on the glass tightened. "She's asleep."

"An hour early! What's wrong? Has she had another asthma attack?"

He could hear the panic rising in Sandra's voice and knew that this was the perfect opportunity to broach the subject of Missi's swimming lessons. "No. She just had a busy day and was tired. We went fishing very early this morning and . . ."

"Sloan, you can't overdo it with her. When she gets tired she's more likely to have an attack."

Suddenly angry, he snapped, "So what if she does? Is it the end of the world if she's having a good time enjoying life?"

"Sloan, you never listen to a word I . . ."

"No, Sandra, for once listen to me. Today, Missi started swimming lessons which I intend to continue while I have her."

A long pause on the other end communicated Sandra's anger more than any words could.

Finally she said, "What are you trying to do, Sloan? Put our daughter in the hospital?"

"The right word is *our*. I'm glad you finally acknowledged that fact, Sandra. I hope when she returns to Atlanta you will continue the swimming lessons. This particular physical activity is recommended for children with asthma. They have to feel like the other kids, Sandra. Quit trying to put Missi in a plastic bubble." While he was on a roll, he figured he might as well tell her everything. "In fact, Sandra, I think you and Missi should have counseling, so you can learn to handle her asthma better. You're trying to protect Missi too much. What's going to happen when she becomes a teen-ager and rebels? Or an adult and leaves home? Will she be equipped to face the real world?"

"She's my responsibility, Sloan. I can't control what you do with her when you have her, but I'm not giving her lessons when she returns. Don't build up her hopes."

The dial tone greeted Sloan's ear. He held the phone for a minute longer, knowing that he had handled the situation all wrong. He had spoken out of anger, not in a calm, rational manner.

Suddenly he found himself wanting to talk with Kendall, to tell her about his conversation with Sandra. Never before had he wanted to share so much with another human being.

He punched out her number and waited. "Kendall, this is Sloan. I need to talk."

Chapter Seven

𝒟ressed in red shorts and a red-white-and-blue-striped shirt, Kendall was seated at the kitchen table, drinking a cup of coffee, when her grandmother walked into the room and sat down opposite her.

"Are you going over to the fair with Flora and me?" Maria asked, pouring herself a cup of coffee.

"No, Sloan will be here in a few minutes."

A glow of contentment was in Kendall's voice, inducing a curious stare from her grandmother. "You've certainly been seeing a lot of that man lately."

It was hard to put into words the special feelings that were aroused in her when she was with Sloan—a sense of family, a womanliness, a oneness with him. Those feelings were alien to her. Maria and she were a family, but it wasn't the same thing. And she had never felt such a part of Blake's life as she did with Sloan.

Even Missi was coming around slowly. Maybe she was looking at the situation with Missi through rose-colored glasses; perhaps she was just wishing that things were getting better.

"How do you think Missi is doing?" Kendall asked, taking another sip of her coffee, her intent gaze trained on Maria's changing expression.

"In the last three weeks I've seen changes for the better. She's starting to grow up." A bright smile accompanied Maria's words.

Kendall placed her cup back on the table, her grandmother's affirmation generating her own smile. "I think so, too. Your pottery lessons have helped, as well as your guidance."

Maria waved her hand in the air. "I have done nothing, Kendall."

"Don't forget, you raised me," Kendall said with a soft laugh. "Missi wasn't a child who took criticism or even suggestions well a month ago, but now she listens. And she hasn't had any more asthma episodes, even when she received her third and fourth shots. You have spent time with her almost every day and she knows you care about her. To Missi that's important."

"To anyone that's important. I don't want you ever to forget that I love you, Kendall." Maria lowered her gaze and studied her half-full coffee cup, an uncharacteristic hesitation in her manner. "I received an answer from my cousin, Anna, a couple of days ago."

Tension whipped through Kendall. She sat up straight in her chair as though bracing herself for the striking blow.

"I'll be leaving in a few weeks. I have some loose ends to tie up first. Then I'm moving back to the reservation."

"No. You can't!" Kendall felt as if the judge had just pronounced the death sentence. "It's too soon, Grandma."

"It's ten years overdo. Kendall, I'm going, and you will have to face that fact sooner or later." Maria stood, carried her cup to the sink, then turned to leave. "Flora will be here soon to pick me up. I'll see you at the fair."

Stunned, Kendall stared at the kitchen door for a long moment. For the past few weeks, she had forgotten all about her grandmother's wanting to leave. Perhaps she had hoped when her grandmother hadn't said anything that her cousin had said no.

Why am I clinging to my grandmother? Kendall asked herself and immediately knew the answer. If her grandmother left and Sloan left, she would be totally alone—that frightened her more than anything. She needed someone to care for, and she in turn needed someone to care for her.

The swish of the door opening startled her and she glanced up. Sloan stood in the doorway, staring at her, a worried look on his face.

"I met your grandmother as she was leaving with Flora." Sloan quickly advanced into the room, sitting in the chair next to hers. "Something's wrong, Kendall. Please tell me about it."

Sloan and she had seen each other every day for the past two weeks, usually with Missi—but always with other people around them, as if he were deliberately surrounding them with a crowd. For some reason he had been reluctant to be alone with her.

Kendall's frown deepened. "It's just a family problem."

Her tone dismissed the subject, but Sloan wouldn't let it drop. "Why can't you trust me, Kendall? Why do you keep shutting the door in my face when I try to get close?"

She twisted about and stared at him, as though his angry words had jolted her with an electric shock. "I'm sorry, Sloan. It's a habit that's not easily broken."

"Talking about a problem might help. I'm a good listener if you'll give me the chance." His tone lowered to a caressing level as he took her hand within his, as if he could impart some of his strength into her with his touch.

"Where's Missi?" Kendall asked, suddenly realizing the little girl wasn't in the room.

"Amy wanted her to go to the fair with her." A wry grin crept into his features. "They wanted to camp out tonight after the fair, but I vetoed that plan. The stray dog was never found and I don't want Missi or Amy out in the open when there's the possibility the dog could return."

"How did Missi take your answer?"

"Actually pretty well. Instead, I'm letting her spend the night at the Frasers'. Do you realize that it will be the first time Missi has been allowed to stay over with a girl friend?" Sloan shook his head in astonishment. "I can't believe what an abnormal life my daughter has lived. I never thought about it much until Missi threw her arms around my neck and thanked me so enthusiastically. Sandra would never let her because she was afraid Missi would have an asthma episode. I didn't realize that Sandra lived in such fear all the time.''

''To a parent it can be scary to watch your child gasp for each breath, but rarely is asthma a fatal illness.''

''It's not that I won't worry about Missi. But I think more harm will be done if she doesn't go than if she does and has an attack.''

Kendall held up the coffeepot. ''Coffee?''

''Yes, please.''

After getting a cup for Sloan and filling it, she poured some more into hers, maintaining an outwardly calm façade while deciding what to say to Sloan. He was waiting for her to make the next move.

''My grandmother is leaving Spencerville in a few weeks to return to the Indian reservation.'' There, it was out, and it hadn't been so hard to confide in him. ''I don't want her to go, Sloan. She's all the family I have left, and she will be hundreds of miles away.'' *Like you will be soon*, she silently added.

''It's never easy to watch a loved one leave, Kendall. But usually there is nothing we can do, but accept their decision and make the best of it.''

Kendall heard Sloan's voice falter. He was remembering when he had had to say good-bye to Missi and thinking ahead to when he would in two weeks. It was her turn to grasp his hand in comfort.

''All your life, Kendall, your grandmother has been

here for you. Now, I suspect, she's going back to her people for herself.''

"I know. But it doesn't ease the pain.''

"No, but would you want to make your grandmother feel any worse than she already does by not giving her your support?''

Kendall turned her head away, her eyes brimming with tears. What Sloan had said was right and made her feel terrible about her earlier conversation with her grandmother. With his thumb under her chin, Sloan forced her to look at him as a lone tear cascaded down her cheek. He lifted his thumb and wiped all traces of her tear away, his touch gentle and soft.

Then moving forward, he kissed her. "You will not lose your grandmother. You can still call and talk to her or go for a visit.'' His breath merged with hers right before his mouth covered hers in a deep, total possession. "Do you realize after the fair that I will be alone with no one to keep me company? Do you think you could take pity on a lonely man this evening?''

"Maybe,'' she said with a coquettish tilt of her head.

"You mean you're going to keep me dangling all day?''

"One of the first lessons I learned as a girl was to always keep the man guessing.''

"My God, woman, you're a tease!'' he said in mock severity.

Rising, Kendall took their cups to the sink. "Well, if we don't get going, we're going to miss the big event of the day—the judging of the children's art projects.''

"Oh, and I thought you meant the three-legged sack race. You know I'm really looking forward to that." His gaze skimmed suggestively down her length, making it very clear he would enjoy her leg pressed against his.

Walking toward the kitchen door, Kendall teasingly changed the subject. "Were you able to sneak a look at Missi's entry?"

As they left Kendall's house and headed for Sloan's car, he answered, "Nope. She wouldn't let me get near it. She's adamant about it being a surprise. Could you get anything out of Maria?"

"Nope. She's just as adamant about it being a surprise as Missi. I tell you, those two are some pair."

"Bent on driving us crazy with curiosity." With amusement warm in his eyes, Sloan opened the car door for Kendall.

When they arrived at the picnic grounds at Crystal Lake, where the arts-and-crafts fair was being held, the first thing that Kendall noticed was that the crowd was larger than last year, with more unfamiliar faces, and the second thing was that Missi was in the midst of a group of children with Chris and Amy. Missi's face was bright with laughter.

"I have to talk with my grandmother," Kendall said when Sloan had switched off the motor. "I wasn't very understanding earlier when she told me about leaving in a few weeks. I . . ." Her voice trailed off into silence as she stared out the front window, oblivious to the gaiety around her.

Sloan clasped her hand and tightened his fingers

around hers, but said nothing. After a long pause, Kendall continued in a stronger voice, "I owe her my support."

"When I had to say good-bye to Missi, the hardest part was not letting her know how much it was tearing me up inside. All that would have accomplished was forcing her to make a choice when she had no choice. It would have been emotional blackmail."

"I didn't mean to do that to my grandmother. But you're right, I was." A faint smile graced her lips.

He gave her hand a quick squeeze. "Let's go before the festivities begin without us," he suggested.

Sloan's hand cupped her elbow as he guided her toward the picnic table where her grandmother was sitting. His touch was reassuring, a beacon in a stormy sea. When Kendall sat down next to Maria on the wooden bench, Sloan tactfully withdrew to check on Missi.

"I was wrong," Kendall murmured, lifting her downcast eyes to look straight into her grandmother's. "I love you, Grandma, and I owe you so much. I have no right to make things difficult for you."

"Child, our love gives us the right to express our true feelings to each other. But it doesn't necessarily mean we will always agree or do what the other wants. We can talk later. Right now, I think they are judging the eight-to-twelve-year-olds' art projects."

Kendall kissed Maria on the cheek, then stood, assisting her grandmother to her feet. "Not many people have been as lucky as I to have someone like you to talk with for thirty-two years. Now we'll just do it by phone.''

Maria leaned lightly on Kendall's arm that she was grasping as they made their way toward the children's arts-and-crafts displays. "My cousin doesn't have a phone, but we can write."

"No phone?" Kendall murmured, her brows drawing into a frown.

Kendall didn't say anything else, but her doubts and frustrations resurfaced. Did her grandmother's cousin live in primitive conditions? Glancing sidelong, she appraised Maria, whose face was paler than usual. Again Kendall wondered if her grandmother was feeling all right, which only increased her concern.

"Grandma, are you feeling . . ."

"Shh, Kendall. They are about to announce the winners and present the ribbons."

Sloan came up behind Kendall and encircled his arms around her middle, pulling her back against him. He rested his chin on the top of her head. Since he had picked her up for the fair, he had touched her more than he ever had in the past few weeks, and in public as though he were proclaiming to all of Spencerville that she was his. A warm, secure feeling blanketed her as she listened to the winners being announced.

When Missi won second place, Sloan's arm tightened momentarily about Kendall as he whispered, "Missi told me that even if she didn't get a ribbon that it is a red-letter day for her. After the sack race are you going to swim in the lake with us?"

Kendall turned within the loose band of his arms. "You're going to let Missi swim? I thought you weren't going to."

"All the other kids are going to, Chris and Amy. How could I say no when her swimming teacher says she's really learning fast? Besides, we'll be there." His arms fell to his sides, and he brought his hand up to rub the back of his neck. "And it's getting unbearably hot. I may not get out of that water all afternoon."

"Daddy, Kendall, look at my ribbon!" Missi said excitedly, thrusting the ribbon and bowl into Sloan's hand.

Sloan examined both carefully, a broad grin moving over his features as he handed them to Kendall. "Will you let me keep the bowl, Missi? I have a perfect place on my mantel for it."

"Sure."

"Oh, Missi, this is good. No wonder you're proud. You're much better at this than I ever was. I think my grandmother gave up on me, deciding that I hadn't inherited any of her skills."

"I'm going to put this bowl in the car. Then Chris and I are going to watch some of the other kids in the relay race." Missi whirled around and dashed off toward Sloan's car.

"Well, I learned one more thing about you. You're a lousy potter." His dark eyes glittered with amusement as he clasped her hand and they began walking toward the display tables. "Let's check out the crafts before lunch, because after lunch we are going to have to prepare ourselves mentally for the big race."

As they strolled among the tables laden with crafts on display as well as for sale, Flora stopped them. "Kendall, I have someone I would like you to meet. This is Dr. Roberts and his wife, Carolyn. They live in Pine Bluff."

"Please, Phil."

Kendall shook Phil's, then Carolyn's, hand and introduced Sloan while Flora excused herself.

"I asked Mrs. Baker to introduce me to the doctor in Spencerville. I knew your father. In fact, I was originally from around here until my family moved to Little Rock when I was twelve. I still come back every summer to my cabin on the lake."

"You're welcome to stop by the clinic anytime you're here." Kendall assessed the man to be around fifty, a little younger than her father.

Phil Roberts grinned. "I always mean to, but I don't get to come down as often as I wish or stay as long as I want. Crystal Lake is one of my favorite places."

"Well, if you ever think about returning permanently to Spencerville, let me know. I've been looking for an associate for the last year, but it's hard to attract someone to this rural area."

"I'll keep that in mind."

When Carolyn and Phil Roberts walked away, Sloan said, "Maybe he'll take you up on it. Then it would give you more time to spend with me."

"More time! Sloan Hunter, as it is I've spent a lot of the last three weeks with you and it has been damned hard juggling my busy schedule around. Sometimes lately, I haven't known if I'm coming or going."

"But worth every minute of it." His humor was more blatant now. "Anyway, I'm not talking about an hour or two."

"You are insatiable!"

"Guilty, ma'am." He clicked his heels together and bowed his head. "Where you're concerned I am." He reduced his voice to a husky whisper and pulled her toward a large oak tree that afforded some shade and some privacy.

His large, powerful hands framed her face and he studied her for a moment, then dipped his head, his lips settling onto hers to sate his hunger. When they parted, their breath tangled in the small space between them, Kendall's heartbeat mirroring the fast pace of Sloan's.

"For three very long weeks I've been patient, Dr. Kendall Spencer. Now, I want my answer. Will you have dinner *alone* with me tonight?" His voice and the caressing motion of his hands on her back were a study in seduction, enticing her to respond in the affirmative.

"Yes, Dr. Sloan Hunter. I wondered when you would ask."

A positively wicked gleam flared in his midnight-dark eyes. "You mean all those cold showers I had to endure were unnecessary?"

"You tell me," she retorted.

"No, Kendall, I want to know what *you* think, how *you* feel, how *you* respond to my caresses. In short, woman, *everything*."

Kendall sat on a blanket, staring out at the lake as darkness quickly cloaked the landscape. A contented sigh drifted from her lips as she curled her arms around her legs and rested her chin on her knees. It had been a long, tiring day and their relaxed picnic dinner had been a nice way to unwind from their resounding defeat in the sack race and their afternoon spent swimming in the lake.

"It's beautiful, isn't it?" Sloan asked from behind her. He fingered a strand of her hair, then brought it to his lips and kissed it. "Beautiful," he murmured.

"Yes, it is. The fireworks should be starting soon—as soon as it's completely dark," Kendall said a little breathlessly.

Sloan let Kendall's hair fall back into place, his hand trailing down her neck along her shoulder and down her arm until he clasped her hand. Sitting up next to her, he lifted her hand to his mouth and kissed the palm, then each finger.

"I love fireworks." Kendall's voice was a weak thread, barely audible.

"So do I," Sloan whispered, his lips moving to nibble at Kendall's wrist, where he could feel her pulse hammering at a rapid speed. "Kendall, I want to make love to you." His thumb had replaced his mouth and was searing fiery circles in the flesh of her wrist.

Kendall closed her eyes to the world of nature and savored the world of her senses that were marvelously attuned to Sloan, to his unique scent, to his devastating touch, to his warmly rough voice.

"I want you to make love to me, Sloan. I think I've wanted it ever since I was here with you the first time."

The cove would always hold a special place in her

heart. It was their private, secluded haven where she could forget for a time the problems a relationship with Sloan would involve.

The sensuous assault on her senses ceased and she lifted her eyelids fractionally to gaze into Sloan's face. Darkness shrouded his features, but Kendall didn't have to see his face to know of the intense look of desire that would be in his eyes. It saturated the space between them, electrifying the air about them.

Sloan pressed Kendall back onto the blanket, then partially covered her body with his. He crushed his mouth into hers, his tongue invading her mouth. The poignant search was neither gentle nor rough, but an acceptance of the intense, overwhelming emotions that lay between them.

"Kendall, in the beginning I didn't want to become involved, but after getting to know you that first evening, I couldn't shake you from my mind. I think you bewitched me." Sloan rubbed his mouth along hers as he spoke in a husky, passion-filled voice, stimulating her with his urgent longing.

Her lips began their own persuasion, tender and warm as they rivaled his in passion. Coaxing his lips apart, she sought the sweet depth of his mouth in an erotic quest, probing it with a fiery haste.

A tremor quaked through his body. Then suddenly she no longer controlled the kiss. His mouth became a driving force, his tongue fencing with hers, eliciting entry into her hidden cavern. He shifted, bringing her slender frame more intimately in contact with the muscular planes of his body.

She locked her arms about his neck and gave in to the power of his ravishing kiss, relishing the savage passion that had sprung to life in him and was passing into her under the brilliant fury of his claim.

When her lungs felt as though they would burst from lack of air, the fierce onslaught of his mouth softened, and Sloan seized her lower lip between his teeth and nibbled lovingly, gently. Then, leisurely, his tongue outlined her mouth.

Kendall felt as if a potent liquor had entered her bloodstream, suddenly making her very intoxicated with the essence of him. She dissolved under the melting force of his desire for her. Everything about them seemed liquid and in her mind they blended into one identity.

As though he couldn't stand any barriers between them, even clothes, he pulled her knit shirt from her waistband and up and over her head, tossing it to the side. Her shorts and bra quickly followed her shirt. Then he stood and hurriedly shed his own clothes. Kendall felt the burning intensity of his eyes on her, even though darkness completely surrounded them.

Kneeling down next to her on the blanket, he lightly grazed his hand over her stomach before moving it lower to stroke her through the lace of her panties.

Kendall trembled, a moan of immense pleasure coming from deep within her throat. The sensations he was painstakingly building in her were exquisite, unbelievably ecstatic. She thought she would explode.

"Oh, Sloan, please."

"No, baby. I've waited too long to hurry this moment

of ours. I want to explore every delicious inch of you.''
His voice was a rough whisper that spoke of his own
heightened desire.

Slowly, maddeningly, he fingered the waistband of
her panties, then finally slipped his hand inside to caress
her quivering flesh.

Fireworks exploded overhead, brightening the black
sky with reds, blues, greens. The fireworks illuminating
the heavens were the perfect backdrop as Sloan slid her
panties down her legs, then lay upon her, pleasurably
heavy.

While he nipped sensuously at the sensitive column of
her neck, she stroked the corded smoothness of his
shoulders, finally moving her hands over his broad back,
deliberately, insolently torturing him.

His mouth descended, fastening onto a taut nipple and
sucking while his hands traveled lower, teasing her legs
apart.

They came together in wildly frenzied movements, as
though this moment had been distilled in time and
marked for them only. As shuddering bursts of pleasure
bolted through Kendall's body, the sky was lit with the
final dazzling display of exploding rockets.

Sloan called out her name in a hoarse groan, went
rigid, then collapsed on top of her, his breathing labored,
his hand smoothing her hair back from her face, trembling with his intense feelings. Rolling off her, he pulled
her close to his length and together they watched the last
sparks of fireworks sizzle toward earth.

''It's not bells ringing, but if I do say so myself, it's
even better,'' Sloan said, chuckling softly. ''Not many

people see actual fireworks when they make love for the first time. Do you think it's an omen of things to come?''

Kendall ran her hand over his bare chest, marveling at the muscular symmetry and strength of his anatomy. She hesitated answering him, her doubts slowly returning to haunt her.

''Kendall?''

She drew in a quivering breath, the motion of her hand halting. ''What's going to become of this, Sloan? I think I'm falling in love with you, and yet I don't see any future for us. I'm scared.''

His throat constricted at the quavering thread of her voice. He couldn't answer her question because he didn't know himself. He was scared, too, of his intense, tender feelings toward Kendall that were developing at a quickly alarming rate. But there hadn't been any humanly possible way for him to stop himself from wanting her, completely and totally.

When he answered her, his voice wasn't as steady as he had wished. ''I don't know, Kendall. If it makes you feel any better, I'm just as scared. I'm not a person who can commit himself to a woman lightly, and the one time I did, it ended in a divorce. I can't go through that again.''

''To give of yourself is to open yourself up to being hurt. It isn't easy. At least not for me,'' Kendall murmured, sitting up and searching for her clothes.

''Tell me about the man who hurt you. I hear that pain in your voice now.''

After clasping her bra, Kendall slipped her knit shirt over her head. ''I thought I was in love with Blake, but now I don't think I was, not the kind of love that lasts a person's lifetime. But my relationship with him left its scars, mainly because of his accusations of how cold I am."

"Cold?" He laid his hand on her shoulder and tugged her back into his embrace. "Oh, Kendall, you are anything but cold. Warm, responsive, loving are better words to describe you."

His reassurances expunged the last vestige of her doubts about her own femininity. She nestled closer within the security of his arms and began telling him about Blake, the hopes she had had, the foolish dream about their working together in Spencerville. When she was through, she felt a strange sense of lightheadedness, of a burden being lifted from her shoulders.

"Thank you, Kendall."

"For what?" With her teeth, she began toying with the shell of his ear.

"Mmm." He inhaled a deep breath, his hold tightening about her. "Doc, I think you're the insatiable one." He expelled a sharply drawn breath, then continued: "Thank you for trusting me with a part of you. That means a lot to me."

Her hands roamed over his chest again in seductive sureness. "I should be thanking you for listening," she whispered into his ear.

"Will you come back to the cabin with me tonight?"

Kendall was very tempted to accept, but it wouldn't be wise. "No. What if Missi came home unexpectedly? We are just beginning to become friends and I don't want to ruin that. I don't think she would be able to handle the situation.''

He sighed heavily, his hand stroking her arm. ''You're probably right. She's never slept over at a friend's house and it might not work out. But I wanted to wake up with you by my side.''

''Well, we certainly don't have to leave right away. The evening is still young.''

Kendall parted her lips to greet the burning seal of his kiss as he pulled her toward him. ''Very young,'' Sloan murmured against her mouth before hungrily seeking what she had to offer.

Chapter Eight

The sun glinted off the clear water, the intense heat of a July day beating unmercifully down upon Kendall although it was barely ten o'clock in the morning. She sought refuge under a towering oak tree where she sat down on a picnic bench. Scanning the near-empty public pool that didn't open until eleven o'clock, she found Missi with her swimming teacher, finishing up her last private lesson. The next day Missi would be leaving for Atlanta. Sloan and she were to drive Missi to Little Rock to catch her plane, and Kendall didn't relish that task.

Two weeks before, after the fair, Sloan's and her relationship had changed and still she was confused about a lot of things. She couldn't see where their relationship was heading. She had told him at the cove that she thought she was falling in love with him, and now she knew for certain she was in love with Sloan.

Two weeks of being in his company every spare moment had shown her the depth of her feelings for him. She loved him absolutely, thoroughly and completely.

Thank goodness this was a relatively quiet summer because she found herself constantly daydreaming about Sloan when she wasn't with him. Every day she discovered something new about him. If Missi hadn't said something two days before about his birthday coming up, he wouldn't have said anything to her. She had been furious with him until he had looked at her innocently and said that he had forgotten all about his own birthday. Apparently birthdays had never been important in his family. In fact, he told her he couldn't remember ever having had a birthday party when he had been growing up. What a crime, Kendall thought.

That was when she and Maria and Missi had come up with a plan. They would surprise him with a birthday party that evening. Kendall had taken the day off to go shopping with Missi in Little Rock. She had told Sloan that she had wanted some private time alone with his daughter. In truth, they were going shopping for Sloan's birthday present. Then they were returning to Spencerville to decorate her house. Sloan would be stopping by for dinner and to pick up Missi.

Kendall waved to Missi, who was leaving the pool to get dressed. In a few minutes they would leave for the drive into Little Rock, and she was barely able to contain her excitement about Sloan's surprise birthday party. She loved to throw surprise parties! She couldn't wait to see his face!

"Hi, Kendall, I'm ready to go." Missi approached

her, dressed in a yellow sundress that Sloan had bought her when the three of them had visited Hot Springs, Arkansas, the previous weekend.

"I like that dress on you, Missi." They began walking toward Kendall's sedan. "Do you think your father suspects anything?"

Missi giggled. "No. In fact, I think he's forgotten about his birthday again." She slid a mischievous look at Kendall. "And I didn't remind him. Won't Daddy be surprised when he comes to pick me up!"

When they were on the highway heading for Little Rock, Kendall asked, "Do you have any ideas about what to get him?"

"A book on how to fish," Missi immediately answered with a straight face.

Laughter pealed from Kendall's throat. "That he could definitely use. Let's see, he finally did catch a decent size fish two days ago, but I think he could still use a book on how to fish."

"Yeah. He almost lost it bringing it in. I wish you could have seen his face that day, Kendall. I think he was as surprised at catching the fish as the fish must have been at being caught."

The rest of the trip they discussed different gift possibilities, rejecting some, thinking about others. When they had reached the shopping mall on the outskirts of Little Rock, their list had grown to seven items.

"I think we should be able to find something special," Kendall said as she locked the car doors.

They spent the next several hours hunting for some

birthday gifts. Missi ended up buying his favorite cologne and the book on how to fish, while Kendall still hadn't found that special gift that would remind him of his stay on Crystal Lake.

"Let's grab something to eat. Maybe on a full stomach something will strike my fancy for your dad."

After ordering hamburgers, Missi blurted out, "I'm going to miss Spencerville. Do you know, Kendall, I haven't had an asthma attack in weeks? Wait until Mommy hears that. Maybe then she'll let me go swimming with the rest of the kids when I get back home."

Kendall felt uncomfortable discussing Missi's mother because she wanted to say so many things that would only complicate the situation. She had no say over how to raise Missi, and Kendall now knew the helplessness that Sloan felt where Missi was concerned. Even though he was Missi's father, he had little control over how she was being raised.

Kendall forced a bright smile to her face. "I think you're part fish, Missi Hunter. I've never seen a child learn to swim so fast. You were keeping up with Amy after only two weeks of lessons."

At the mention of Amy's name, Missi's pout that had been gone for weeks returned. "Amy's parents asked Daddy if I could stay next week and leave when they had to. He told them no."

Sloan had been upset the whole evening after talking with Sandra, pleading with her to let Missi stay the extra week with her new friend. He had assured Sandra that the Frasers, who were both teachers in Fort Smith, Arkansas, were nice, decent people.

But Sandra wanted Missi home, where she could keep an eye on her and undo some of the things that Sloan had done, Sandra had told him. For the rest of the evening Sloan had been tied up in knots, saying very little, dreading the time he had to tell Missi no. Kendall had wanted to erase the pain in his eyes, but there was nothing she could say that would change the situation.

"Your mother hasn't seen you in six weeks. She's anxious to have you home." Kendall toyed with her paper napkin in her lap, twisting it, then untwisting it until it was shredded.

The rest of the late lunch Kendall steered Missi away from the subject of returning home. When they had finished their hamburgers, they headed for the other end of the mall. As they passed an art gallery, an oil painting in the window caught Kendall's eye. It was of Crystal Lake, painted as if the artist had sat on the shore and gazed out onto the lake, almost the same view as from "their cove." Kendall had to have that picture! Sloan could take a little of Crystal Lake back with him to St. Louis.

Quickly Kendall entered the gallery and inquired about the oil painting. Ten minutes later she and Missi left the shop with Kendall carrying the picture. They made their way to the car, their anticipation of the evening's events beginning to build.

When they returned to Spencerville it was after six and Sloan was to come over at seven for dinner. The guests—the Frasers, Chris, Bonnie and her husband, Kirk, who was Spencerville's sheriff—were to be at Kendall's house at six-forty-five.

Maria already had everything prepared for dinner. But she had left the decorating for Kendall and Missi to do. As they strung the streamers and hung the banner, they speculated on what Sloan would say and do when he walked through the front door.

At six-thirty Kendall excused herself to freshen up and change into a red backless sundress. She only had a few more days with Sloan and she wanted everything to be perfect.

A few more days. At the realization, she sank onto her bed, her legs suddenly weak, her hands trembling as she lifted one to brush some imaginary strands of hair from her face.

Sloan would be leaving for St. Louis Sunday night. Would he ever call her? Would she ever see him again? He hadn't said much about the future and she had been afraid to bring up the subject.

Her heart throbbed painfully. The hurt was already beginning and he hadn't even left yet. What would she do when he was gone? Fall apart?

People's voices from the living room jolted her from her self-pity and she gathered her poise about her. She wouldn't ruin this last weekend with Sloan by feeling sorry for herself.

Taking a deep breath, she pushed herself off the bed and walked from her bedroom to greet the arriving guests. At seven all the guests were hidden in the kitchen and Missi and Kendall were sitting in the living room, waiting impatiently for Sloan to arrive.

Five minutes later Kendall heard a car door slam closed and she surged to her feet, quickly covering the distance to the door before Sloan had ascended the porch steps. She smoothed her dress, then flung open the front door, a brilliant smile of welcome on her face.

His smile equaled hers in brightness. "Do you realize I was supposed to work all day on that report I've been putting off the whole vacation, and I didn't get two pages done! The cabin was too quiet with you two in Little Rock."

Sloan drew Kendall into his arms and planted a firm kiss on her mouth that tilted her balance. She clutched at his shoulders to steady herself. She wanted the kiss to go on forever, but the knowledge that the house was full of guests quashed the impulse. Pulling away, she backed into the house, drawing him into the living room, where Missi was standing surrounded by all their party decorations.

Sloan's dark eyes widened, his mouth opening slightly in surprise. Stunned, he scanned the room, then returned his attention to Kendall.

"Happy birthday, Sloan!" Kendall said loudly.

People flooded the room, all congratulating him on being a year older. Sloan was at a loss for words, but when Missi threw herself into his arms, he finally snapped out of the dazed state he had been in.

"Was this your idea, hon?" Sloan asked Missi as he placed her back on the floor.

"Kendall's, but I helped her plan it," Missi answered proudly. "Wait till you see what I got you today, Daddy."

"But you can't open any presents until after dinner.

Missi and I worked hard today setting this up, and I'm starved." Kendall linked her arm through his to lead him through the kitchen and into the backyard.

"Woman, I've always said you have an insatiable appetite." His devilish grin promised pure, delightful sin later when they were alone.

"And I can't wait to eat the barbecued chicken Grandma has cooking on the grill out back," she whispered as they stepped outside and descended the steps.

Everyone helped himself to the chicken, potato salad, rolls and corn on the cob, then found a seat on the grass or in the chairs on the covered patio. Amy, Chris and Missi ate under the pecan tree away from the adults.

Many varied topics of conversation flowed freely around the group of adults on the patio, with everyone offering his opinion on the state of the economy, on the recent presidential tour to Europe, on the next season for the Arkansas Razorbacks.

"Do you teach any classes at the university, Sloan?" Bonnie asked, finishing the last of her dinner and placing the plate on the redwood picnic table.

"A couple of graduate courses. Most of my time is spent in the laboratory working as head of a research project."

"Oh, what kind of project do you work on?" Kirk asked.

"Cancer of the lungs." Sloan smiled toward Kendall, who sat next to him on a double redwood glider. "There was a time that I wanted to be a doctor like Kendall, but I decided I would become too emotionally involved with my patients to be any good for them. I don't know how Kendall does it. I have great admiration for doctors of medicine." His hand covered Kendall's, his fingers curling over hers. "So, instead I decided to work on cures for diseases. I thought I could handle beakers, chemicals and test tubes better." Amusement, directed at himself, laced his voice.

"Speaking of doctors, Kendall," Bonnie said, "Dr. Roberts stopped by after you left this morning and I gave him the grand tour of the clinic. He was very impressed. For a small rural town he felt we had quite a lot of equipment to handle many types of emergencies."

"I'm sorry I missed him." The feel of Sloan's hand over hers suffused her body with a languorous heat that made her want to nestle closer in his arms and go to sleep. "Did he say if he would be able to come back some other time?"

"Not for a few months. He's leaving tomorrow. His son was coming home for a few days before he began his internship."

"Well, it looks like everyone has finished eating," Sloan said, looking pointedly at Kendall. "What should we do now, Doc?"

"Oh, I don't know. We have horseshoes set up in the back or we could play croquet."

Sloan snapped his fingers. "I've got an idea. Why don't I open my presents?"

"For someone who forgot his own birthday, you sure are getting into the swing of things," Kendall said with a laugh.

"I can only be patient about some things." Humor was deep in his dark eyes.

Kendall blushed as she rose to get the presents from the living room. She could vividly remember his "patience"; he had painstakingly knocked down every barrier she had erected against him.

"Do you need any help?" Maria asked, starting to get up.

Kendall waved her back into her seat. "No, Grandma, you've done enough. Bonnie will help me." She had to keep reminding herself that her grandmother was eighty years old and was not as capable of doing everything around the house as she used to be. It was hard, though, since Kendall had always thought of her grandmother as young and vital. But the lines of age on Maria's face had become more pronounced, and her bright, brown eyes were not as sparkling as before.

Inside the house, Kendall stacked several presents for Bonnie to carry outside to the patio. "You should have brought Lisa and Mark."

"Are you kidding? This is our one night out without the kids. Besides, Lisa is at the age when she's into everything. And I mean *everything!* Take, for instance, these beautifully wrapped packages. In one minute they would have been destroyed."

"But, Bonnie Phillips, you wouldn't trade your family for anything." Kendall placed the stacked presents in Bonnie's outstretched arms.

"No way! It's not easy working full-time and being a mother of two, especially when they are both under six, but if you want something badly enough, you're willing to make compromises to have it. And it makes you work that much harder to make sure it all works out.'' Bonnie shifted the presents to a more comfortable position, her sharp gaze drilling into Kendall. ''This evening you've hardly taken your eyes off Sloan. You're pretty serious about him, aren't you?''

''Yes,'' was Kendall's quiet reply. *Very serious,* she added silently.

''What are you two going to do when he has to leave on Sunday?''

The question Kendall had tried to avoid the previous two weeks charged the suddenly tense atmosphere. Bonnie had spoken of compromises in a relationship, but what kind of compromise could they reach? Sloan hadn't even said he loved her, and even if he did, the work that they both loved and was a part of them made it necessary to live in two different states.

''I wish I knew, Bonnie.'' Kendall tried to smile, to laugh off a threatening depression. ''I think I've gotten myself into a fine mess.''

Bonnie started to say something when they heard the kitchen door bang closed. ''What's keeping you two?'' Sloan appeared in the doorway, looking boyishly eager.

''Coming. Coming,'' Bonnie called out. Then she whispered as she walked past Kendall, ''If you need to talk Monday, I'll be available.''

When Bonnie had left, Sloan narrowed his eyes and fixed a stern expression on his face that couldn't quite wipe away his silent laughter. ''What's the conspiracy?''

Kendall mentally shook off her troubling thoughts and answered lightly, ''We were wondering how in the world you were ever going to blow out all your candles. The cake's going to look like it's on fire."

"Funny, Doc. Just wait until *you* turn thirty-three."

"I'll meet you outside. I have one more present to get."

He pinned her beneath the smoldering cinders of his eyes. "Yours?"

She nodded, unable to take her eyes from his. It was as if he were making love to her with them, stripping away her clothes and touching every inch of her.

"Well, in that case I'll help you."

"No," she protested in a weak voice. She leaned back, half-sitting on the couch, clutching at it for support.

"Somehow I get the feeling I should open your present in private, Kendall."

Without a word Kendall walked into the den and retrieved the wrapped picture from behind the chair that was situated in the far corner. Sloan was right. She didn't want to share the moment with anyone.

"I hope you like it," Kendall murmured, easing into the chair while he lifted the large package.

He pretended to shake it. "I don't think it's jewelry or a book." But when his laughter-filled eyes beheld Kendall's wide, sober gaze, all teasing fled from his expression. In that moment, he knew the present she had selected for him held a deep meaning. He sat opposite her and began carefully unwrapping the gift.

When the last of the wrapping paper fell away to reveal the painting, Kendall waited anxiously for Sloan's reaction. His intent look took in every inch of the oil canvas, picturing the lake at sunset. His smile was slow, but full of a knowing warmth that bound them invisibly together.

"I don't know what to say, Kendall," Sloan said, looking up.

"Do you like it?" she inquired cautiously, hoping the painting would hold a deep meaning for him as well.

"I have a special place to hang this painting, and when I look at it, I will always remember the beautiful time we spent together at the cove." His voice, slightly unsteady, weakened even more and he fell silent.

Suddenly so many things needed to be said. "Sloan, we have to talk about . . ."

"There you two are. I thought you all were supposed to be following me outside." Bonnie stood in the doorway with her hands on her hips. "Don't tell me you've forgotten all about opening your presents, Sloan! What have you been doing in here? Starting without the rest of us?"

Sloan rallied first, smiling as he rose. "Now, come on, Bonnie, surely you're a romantic at heart. You can't blame a guy for wanting a few minutes alone with his girl. After all, this is supposed to be *my* day."

"Not when all of us have been dying of curiosity for the last ten minutes," Bonnie retorted.

Sloan extended one hand to help Kendall to her feet while holding the painting in his other one. He briefly squeezed her hand before they followed Bonnie outside to the patio. "We'll talk later when there aren't so many people around," Sloan whispered into Kendall's ear as he held the back door for Bonnie and her.

All of a sudden, though, Kendall wasn't feeling as brave as when they were in the den. She wished she could forget that Sloan was leaving on Sunday and that a future between them was in grave doubt. But she couldn't. She tried to join in on the fun as Sloan opened each present, most of them gag gifts, but even though she laughed in all the appropriate places, it sounded forced to her ears.

After Sloan opened his birthday gifts, Maria served cake and ice cream, Kirk declaring Sloan would never be able to blow out all the candles in one breath. As everyone was singing "Happy Birthday," Sloan threw back his head, inhaled a deep breath, then blew out all the candles, looking up triumphantly when the last one flickered out.

"You all should never have doubted a guy with so much hot air," Sloan quipped as he sliced himself a huge piece of chocolate cake, announcing to the group that he was a chocolate addict. "If you all don't get your piece fast, there won't be any left." He grinned broadly.

Chris, then the Frasers, left after the dessert, while Maria and Missi retired to the kitchen to start cleaning up, leaving Sloan and Kendall to take down the decorations. Standing on the front porch, their arms linked around each other's waist, Kendall and Sloan said good-bye to the last guests, Bonnie and Kirk.

When they had driven away, Sloan brought his free arm around to completely encircle Kendall in a loose embrace. Darkness shrouded them like a heavy warm blanket, the moon's light obscured by drifting clouds.

"That was some surprise, lady." The loose embrace

tightened as he urged her closer, fitting her slim length against his hard planes. "Doc, I have so many things to say to you that I'm not sure where to begin."

"Well, why don't you start . . ."

"At the beginning," Sloan finished for her, a deep laughter ringing in his voice. "I set myself up for that one."

"That's not a bad place to begin, but that wasn't what I was going to say."

"What were you going to say?"

She could imagine the mocking lift of one eyebrow, the teasing curve of his mouth. "It's too late now. My lips are sealed. That's what you get for not letting me finish." Even though he wouldn't be able to see, Kendall compressed her lips into a thin, straight line.

"Oh, no, you don't, Kendall Spencer." With a punishing swiftness he ravaged her mouth with a fierce kiss, forcing his tongue between her tightly drawn lips only to come up against her barrier of clamped teeth. Pushing away slightly, he chuckled arrogantly, as though he knew it was futile to fight him. "Doc, don't make me use my ultimate weapon."

Kendall freed herself and started backing away. "Ultimate weapon?" she queried in a half-whisper, then laughed, her own laughter full of self-assurance. "I'm not that easily intimidated, Sloan Hunter. I'll tell you only if I'm good and ready."

His long strides quickly carried him toward her before she had a chance to escape. Suddenly, she found herself trapped with the porch swing to her back and to her front Sloan, ready to block any avenue of retreat. With a gentle nudge, he pushed her down onto the swing, his huge body towering over her. As swift as a jungle cat, he was next to her, his muscular arms imprisoning her between him and the back of the seat.

"You have one last chance, Kendall." Laughter threatened to steal his voice. "Well?"

"Sloan, do I need to answer?"

Before she realized his intent, he pinned her against him and was unmercifully tickling her. She was laughing so hard that tears began to trickle down her cheeks.

"Okay, Sloan," she called out between gasps for air.

Suddenly their nearness altered the atmosphere between them, a sexual tension enveloping them and sharply focusing all their senses on the other. Sloan closed in on her, dropping light kisses along the wet path of her tears. He kissed her everywhere on her face but her mouth, and soon Kendall discovered that the intense yearning to be claimed was Sloan's *real* ultimate weapon.

She grasped his head in her hands and brought his mouth down on hers, denying herself nothing as she tasted of him. "I love you, Sloan Hunter," she murmured when their mouths were no longer in contact, when their quickening breath blended.

"That's the best birthday present anyone has ever given me. I know you want assurances that everything is going to work out for us, and I wish I could give them to you. But all I know is I love you totally and completely and I pray to God there is a way we can work out a future for us."

Kendall wanted to ask how but was afraid to voice

aloud all her doubts, not when he was holding her so tenderly and nibbling on her ear. There would be time later when they had to say good-bye.

The sound of Missi's laughter from inside the house separated them and they had just straightened on the swing when Missi came bounding out onto the porch ahead of Maria.

"We've finished the dishes, Daddy. But you and Kendall haven't taken down one decoration yet."

"I hated to spoil your work of art," he teased, tugging Missi down onto his lap and hugging her. "I guess I'd better do my job before we've got to get home to pack all your things."

Missi twisted around to ask, "Maria, will you go with Sloan and Kendall to see me off at the airport tomorrow?"

"No, my child. I don't like saying good-bye. I'd rather do it here tonight." There was a sad smile in Maria's voice.

For a few seconds Kendall felt as if her heart had stopped beating. She hated good-byes, too, and yet on Sunday evening she would have to say her most difficult good-bye of all.

Chapter Nine

Sloan's hands were rammed into the pockets of his brown trousers as he stared out the large window while Missi's plane taxied out to the runway. The solemn expression on his face concealed the pain Kendall knew he was feeling. The parting scene between him and Missi tore at her heart. Sloan and Missi knew they wouldn't see each other until Christmastime, six months away. They both would have to content themselves with letter-writing and telephoning, but somehow that would never be enough for either one of them.

Kendall certainly knew that wouldn't be enough for herself. Soon it would be her turn to say good-bye to Sloan and she would have to settle for the same thing as Missi. Her heart went out to the little girl, who had thrust a wrapped package into her hands just before getting on the plane. Kendall still held the package, clutched in her hand, unopened.

Swallowing away the tightness in her throat, Kendall searched for something to say to Sloan that would help ease the hurt. But her mind was blank. She reached out to touch Sloan's shoulder but hesitated, her hand wavering in the air a few inches away from him.

Perhaps she should leave him alone for a while. Maybe he didn't want her near him while he wrestled with his feelings, his guilt. But as though her hand had a will of its own, it lay heavily upon his shoulder, automatically kneading the corded muscles beneath her fingertips.

Sloan covered her hand with his. "I'm glad you're here, Kendall. It makes it easier not having to face this alone. At Christmas I left a crying, very unhappy child on the plane. It took all my willpower not to snatch her up into my arms and carry her off the plane. This time at least I know she had a happy time and has learned to face a few realities." He turned around to face her, his sadness revealed in his eyes.

"You know, I haven't even opened the present she gave me." Kendall attempted to interject some lightness into the situation, but it fell short.

"I think you'll like it."

"You know what it is?"

He nodded, gesturing toward two seats that were facing away from the picture window.

Kendall's ripping into the wrapping paper produced a chuckle from Sloan. "You certainly don't believe in saving the wrapping."

"No way. One of the best parts of getting a gift is opening the present."

"But Missi really took her time wrapping that gift for you. She wanted everything to look just right," he chided her gently, but the laugh lines at the corners of his eyes deepened as he watched her expression when she opened the box.

"It's beautiful," Kendall murmured, holding up a clay bowl that Missi had made that matched Sloan's. Her throat closed and she had a difficult time keeping herself from crying in a public place.

"Do you think she's trying to tell us something?"

"That she approves of us now?"

"Yes."

Kendall looked beyond Sloan toward the plane, then back at him. "I know that we became friends in these last few weeks. We talked about her asthma and things she could do to help herself. I think since that asthma episode in my office she didn't see me as quite the ogre she thought I was at first." Kendall's expression clouded, her eyes darkening. "But I won't kid myself. If the opportunity arose for you and Sandra to get back together, she would want that more than anything. It's only natural."

"Come on. Let's get out of here. I know of a nice restaurant that the Frasers told me about. We'll have an early dinner, then drive back to the cabin." Sloan stood, pulling Kendall to her feet. "Will you stay the night, Kendall?"

Without hesitation, she answered, "Yes."

It wasn't until after they had placed their orders at the

restaurant that the subject of their own separation was brought up. Running his fingers up and down the stem of his wineglass, Sloan said, "I'll have to leave by five tomorrow evening, Kendall. It's almost eight hours to St. Louis, and I have to be in the laboratory by eight Monday morning for a conference with my staff."

Five o'clock Sunday was less than twenty-four hours away, Kendall thought with a rising panic. "What are we going to do, Sloan? It won't be easy for us to see each other."

"I've been giving it a lot of thought the last few days. We'll just have to make time, Kendall. Neither one of us can leave our jobs. Besides, we could never ask that of the other. We both have commitments to our work that can't be lightly dismissed."

"After the summer months I might be able to come to St. Louis for a long weekend in September."

"And it's possible I could arrange a few days in August. We'll work things out."

How long do we take it one day at a time? Kendall couldn't help but wonder. There would come a time when a decision about the future had to be made. She didn't know how she would handle seeing him a few days every once in a while. She had never taken things lightly and certainly couldn't take their relationship that way. But she didn't voice her doubts. She would take anything right now, even a few days.

They quickly ate their steak and lobster dinner because they were both eager to return to the cabin. Suddenly neither one wanted anyone else around. They had only one day and they wanted to spend it completely alone with each other.

On the drive back to Spencerville, Kendall sat next to Sloan, who was driving her sedan. She was glad they had taken her car because his sports car had bucket seats. She savored the quiet closeness they shared, the silence neither uncomfortable nor tense.

Pulling up to the cabin, Sloan turned off the engine, then twisted around to face Kendall. "Some dark clouds are moving in from the south, but the sun's setting. I'd like to walk along the lakeshore one last time with you."

A coldness swept through Kendall, as though those words were an omen. It took her a moment to compose herself and to dismiss her uneasy feelings.

She fitted her hand within his. "I'd like that, too."

"When I see a sunset, I'll always think of you," Sloan said as they strolled under the tall pines and oaks that wooded the shoreline.

"Dazzling, all red and purple," Kendall kidded. If she didn't tease him, she was afraid she might break down and cry. She felt split in two. She wanted to be with him right now, and yet when she was with him, she realized all she would be missing when he left. The lonely heartache was beginning to creep up on her, and she battled to hold it at bay.

"No, beautiful to watch. Haven't you ever wanted to reach out and touch something awe-inspiring in nature? With you, I feel I have."

"Don't, Sloan." Kendall halted, her eyes closed against the sight of him and the sunset.

"Don't what?" He touched her arm that hung stiffly at her side.

She flinched away, opening her eyes but looking beyond Sloan at the lake, the light fading quickly as the dark clouds were carried across the sky. "I don't think I can handle the compliments right now. I don't want our last day together to be serious."

He captured her face in his powerful hands and forced her to look at him. "But I want you to know how I feel about you. I love you, Kendall Spencer. Our relationship isn't going to be smooth, but I think we're worth fighting for. I grant you we have a problem that most couples don't have, but things will work out for us."

"Dammit, how?" She finally shouted the question she had been wanting to ask ever since she knew she was in love with him.

"I don't know!" His voice was equally loud, tense.

Kendall stared at Sloan for a long moment, the frustration mounting.

"Maybe we should end it now before we get in any deeper and really hurt each other." She finally said what she had been thinking for days now.

"No!" he replied in a harsh voice, but immediately his expression softened and he drew her to him, burying his face in her hair. "Then we would always wonder if it could have worked. I'm already in deep, Kendall, and the only way I can see not ending up being hurt is to try it and make it work for us."

Wrapping her arms about him, she laid her head on his chest and listened to the quick beat of his heart. What

Sloan had said was true. If she walked away now, she would be hurt terribly; that was a sure fact. The other alternative gave them a small chance at happiness and she would be a fool not to accept it.

Enclosed within his warm embrace, Kendall felt the first drops of rain. They pulled apart, laughing. Sloan's arm went about her shoulder, and instead of making a run for the cabin, they began walking away from it, further down the shore.

The summer shower was gentle and soothing. Kendall lifted her face and gloried in the feel of the light rain on her skin. At some point they turned and headed back toward the cabin, but Kendall was oblivious to her surroundings. She thought only of the moment with Sloan next to her, his warmth saturating her heart with his essence. She felt in that instant she would explode with her desire for him, and she finally sought to hurry their pace. The next twenty hours would have to last her a long time, and she was hungry to explore and memorize every inch of him.

Inside the dry shelter of the cabin, they parted and suddenly Kendall was cold from her soaked, clinging dress. His raking gaze made a thorough, leisurely study of her, noting the wet, black curls that framed her face, her gray eyes, almost silver with her desire for him, her breathing that was becoming more rapid the longer he stared at her, and her dress that was molded to the slender curves of her body in a very provocative way. Finishing his sensuous survey, he returned his ardent attention to her face, his slow smile packed with a

compelling male charm that sharpened his surging cha-
risma that kept drawing Kendall to him over and over,
even against her better judgment.

A lazy look of wickedness stole over his face when he
spoke in a low tone of seduction. "It's been a long day.
Don't you think it's time we retire for the night?"

He extended his hand and Kendall settled hers within
his large one. Inside his bedroom he turned in toward
her, cupping her face as his penetrating dark eyes
regarded her with an intentness that drove the breath
from her. Leaning forward, he sampled her lips in a
tentative exploration that quickly burst into a ravenous
claim. His hands moved from her face to her shoulders
until they rested right below her waist, gently pressing
her closer to him. Kendall was achingly aware of his
every sinewy muscle which seemed to mold itself
against her, becoming a part of her own body.

Slowly, while still holding her close to him, he
unzipped her dress. Stepping slightly away, Sloan eased
each strap off her shoulders and down her arms until her
dress lay in a pool at her feet. Boldly, she matched his
steady appraisal as he took in her lovely body, dressed
only in a half-slip and panties. Her nipples stiffened
under the zealous heat of his regard, and she moistened
her suddenly dry lips with a suggestive movement of her
tongue. She felt as if she were being consumed inch by
inch by the power of his look, her senses vibrating with
her longing to be one with him.

Without breaking the visual thread between them,
Sloan unbuttoned his shirt, revealing his massive chest,
still damp from the rain. Then, as if he were suddenly in

a hurry, he shed his clothes and stood before her, his sheer masculine beauty elemental and overwhelming.

Sloan quickly laced his hands through the damp tangles of her hair, pulling her to him. He brushed light, fleeting kisses again and again over her lips while his thumb stroked her earlobe into sexual arousal. She ached for him to deepen his kisses, her body aflame with wanting him, her passion as strong and unrestrained as his.

Finally he sought the moist fragrance of her lips, and she opened them to receive his questing tongue that made delicious circles inside her mouth. Her fingers probed the rich thickness of his hair while urging him nearer. His lips were persuasively demanding as the kiss lengthened, Kendall headily conscious of his male warmth and his subtle scent.

Sloan raised his head, severing their thrilling joining, and scooped her up into his arms. With fluid movements, he strode to his bed and gently lay Kendall in the center of it. He straightened, his eyes singeing her. Kneeling, he ran his finger along the waistband of her half-slip. Then in one quick motion he removed her last garments, as though his patience had finally been exhausted.

With infinite care, his hands roamed over her, and she closed her eyes for a sweet moment to savor the rapturous warmth of his caresses. He bent over, his mouth following the same path of delightful inquiry, finally pausing to excite first one nipple, then the other, into peaks of hardness with quick flicks of his tongue.

Kendall moaned, arching her body beneath the touch

of his mouth, which was bringing each part of her to white-hot readiness, as if she were being bathed in a liquid fire.

Sloan lifted his head and seized her rapt attention with the fiery look of desire in his eyes. ''I need you so much, my love.''

His husky words pierced through the haze of ecstasy, their meaning slicing through her to her very soul, where she would treasure them forever. Her eyes spoke a message of her needs, her love, and Sloan stretched out along beside her, half covering her with his body. He pulled her into the tight circle of his arms and hugged her to him. A new certainty of the other was conveyed in their embrace, bringing a magic to the moment.

With a special kind of tenderness evolved from a deep-felt love, Sloan touched every place he knew aroused her, inducing exquisite pleasure. Parting her legs, he stroked her inner thighs, and a wave of blissful sensations roared through her, eliciting from her a fevered response.

She commanded with gripping hands that he love her, fill her with his being. Everything was traveling at a dizzying speed, pushing her faster and faster toward a plane of total, complete fulfillment.

Afterward, it took a long time for her to float back down to reality. Sloan rolled off her, then drew her to him. Only then did she become aware of her surroundings while still glorying in the unique experience they had shared.

And tomorrow evening he will be gone. The disturbing

thought came unbidden into her mind, chilling her. She shuddered and Sloan cradled her closer, pulling a sheet over them.

"I don't want us to get sick because of our walk in the rain," he murmured against her hair.

"Sloan, I love you." Her voice almost sounded desperate.

"I know, darling." His hand began to caress her with a newfound sureness that only a deep closeness in spirit could produce. "Go to sleep, love."

Sloan sat in the chair in his bedroom, staring at Kendall's sleeping form. He never thought he would experience what he had shared with Kendall the night before. In fact, for many years he had given up on love, the kind of special feeling he had toward Kendall.

His expression saddened as his thoughts were inundated with what lay ahead for them. She had asked him how things were going to work. Truthfully, he didn't really know how he was going to make it through each day without her. He had come to depend on her for support, advice.

For a brief moment he played with the idea of leaving his post at the university and moving to Spencerville. But he knew in his heart he would never be the same man if he backed out of a commitment. It would grow and fester within him and soon drive a wedge between them just as it would if she left Spencerville to live in St. Louis.

But, dammit, it wasn't fair! Sloan slammed his fist

into the arm of the chair, then quickly stood, pacing restlessly about the room. He had slept no more than one hour, only then because he had been so tired that he had drifted into a light sleep. He hadn't wanted to because he needed to remember everything about their last day together. He hadn't wanted to lose one conscious minute of the time left to him.

He paused at the window that overlooked the wooded area and the lake in the distance. Jamming his hands into the pockets of his velour robe, he went over and over the past five weeks. Could he have done something different because the dull ache he was feeling was intensifying as five o'clock grew nearer? No, he acknowledged to himself. From the first time he had seen Kendall, he had been attracted to her and that attraction had only magnified.

How am I going to get in my car and drive away from her? Sloan wondered as he watched the gray light of dawn blossom into a new day.

I really have no choice.

The sheets rustled behind him, and he thought of all the mornings he wouldn't wake up with her beside him.

A vague coldness caused Kendall to shiver and she shifted from her back to her side. Slowly her eyelids fanned open and the first thing she noticed was the empty place where Sloan had been. The second thing was his tall frame silhouetted against the bright sunlight cascading through the window. He stood deathly still, as though every muscle in his body was paralyzed.

She wondered what he was feeling as the evening

approached. Time was moving too fast for her. She wanted to change the laws of nature and halt the progression of time; she wanted this day never to end; she wanted their whole existence to be this one cabin. She wanted a lot of things.

She had only said good-bye to one person who had been important in her life—her father. Blake had angered her, hurt her with his cruel accusations, but very quickly she had learned he had meant little to her, that he had always taken from their relationship and never given. But in the short time she had known Sloan, she knew she would have to say her second good-bye that evening.

Somewhere within herself she would have to find the strength to make it through the day without a big emotional scene. She had never considered herself to be emotional until Sloan had awakened in her feelings that she hadn't known existed. As a doctor she had been trained to be disciplined, to remove herself emotionally from pain, but she was finding it difficult now to do either.

Kendall twisted around and lay on her back, stretching her arms over her head while pointing her toes. After the previous night she realized that no other man would be able to take Sloan's place in her life. She was determined more than ever to grab what she could and just maybe things would work out for them someday.

That's the attitude, Kendall, she told herself as she sat up in bed, the movement drawing Sloan's attention.

He turned and smiled at her, an almost shy smile. "Good morning, Doc."

"That it is," she answered in a flippant tone, stretching again as though she were a satisfied cat.

Sloan moved quickly and sat on the bed next to her. "Did you sleep well?"

"Quite. But, Sloan, you sound embarrassed. I'm the one who isn't used to waking up with a man in my room."

"To tell you the truth, I'm not either."

He grinned devilishly and his meaning was very apparent. She struck him playfully on the arm. "Sloan Hunter, you know what I mean!"

Sloan threw back his head and let his laughter roll from deep within his chest. "Yes, I know what you mean. To tell you the truth, I was usually long gone when Sandra would wake up in the morning."

Without any warning, Sloan hauled her around to lie half in his lap and half on the bed, his arms trapping her deliciously against the hard male contours of his body. He planted several breathy kisses on her lips, punctuating each one with, "I love you, Doc."

Then he moved his teasing attention to her ear, where he nipped gently at its shell. Quickly Kendall was losing all control.

It didn't take much for them to end up lying on the bed, entwined within each other's arms, renewing their intimate knowledge of the other. Again Kendall journeyed down the wonderfully ecstatic path like the night before, but this time her fingers grazed him in teasing, suggestive torment. This time her hands and mouth searched out his sensitive points that brought him to a fevered pitch.

Later when their ragged breathing had slowed to a normal rate and the pounding of their hearts no longer drummed in their ears, Kendall looked at him questioningly. "What do you have planned for today?"

"First a shower, then breakfast. I've discovered lying in bed makes me very tired. Then after breakfast, who knows? Maybe we might test out this bed a little more. When I return to St. Louis, I'm sure Carl will want to know what I thought about his cabin. I . . ."

The mention of St. Louis made her stiffen. The sudden silence pulsated between them. One minute. Two minutes.

"I didn't mean to bring that up," Sloan said finally.

Kendall forced her features into a neutral expression while inside she was shattered. Bracing herself with one elbow, she looked down at him. "We can't avoid the subject all day, Sloan. Somewhere in our conversations we will mention our separate lives. It's only natural. I don't want our last day together to be a constant battle not to say this or only talk about that."

He lifted his hand and wound a strand of her hair around a finger, then brought it toward his mouth, kissing the strand in a gentle gesture. "Let's take that shower."

"Together, in that small stall!"

"Where's your romantic spirit, Doc. Yes, together in that small stall." A mischievous imp took over, hauling her from the bed and toward the bathroom.

From the moment Kendall stepped into the shower stall, she couldn't contain her laughter. They barely fit, which pleased Sloan to no end. But when he went to wash himself, he kept hitting his elbow on the wall.

"Ouch! I'm going to have to tell Carl his shower isn't made for two people."

"Won't that open up a can of worms?" Watching Sloan struggle with the cramped space, Kendall added, "Let me do that for you."

She took the washcloth from his hand and soaped it, then ran it vigorously over his back before turning him around—which was no easy feat—and cleansing his chest, arms and neck.

"Now it's my turn," Sloan announced.

"But I haven't finished."

"That's okay. I'll have the cleanest upper half in town. Frankly, Doc, I can't take much more of this torture. You were right about this not being big enough for two. Your body is driving me crazy. At this rate we'll never have breakfast. We should have used the bathtub. No, on second thought, that wouldn't have been much better."

Suddenly Kendall reveled in the power she had over him. He wanted her as much as she wanted him and that knowledge was like an aphrodisiac. Sloan Hunter had taught her that she was a very warm, responsive woman, and she would always be in his debt for that.

With a saucy smile on her face, she rubbed against him, delighting in the feel of his wet skin against hers. That was all the temptation Sloan needed to drop the washcloth on the floor of the stall and to take Kendall into his arms.

"The hell with breakfast, woman." His low growl aroused her as much as his hands roving over her back. "I've never done it standing up, but with you I want to experience everything."

Time came to a standstill as the water beat down upon them, clasped in a lovers' embrace. It wasn't until an hour later that they were in the kitchen finally attempting to fix breakfast.

"One of us has got to learn to cook, lady." Sloan cracked an egg into the frying pan and broke the yolk, the third one.

"Any volunteers?" Kendall retorted, pouring the orange juice.

After finally successfully cracking two eggs, Sloan turned around with a spatula in his hand. "We'll have to draw straws, then."

"We could always eat out or not eat."

"No good. Now, let me see. I bought a box of straws for Missi and I think some are left." Sloan scooped the eggs out of the frying pan, then began rummaging through the cabinets until he triumphantly produced a near-empty box. He cut off a long piece and a short one. Then twisting away from Kendall he placed both of them in his fist before facing her again. "Whoever gets the short one has to take cooking lessons."

Kendall glanced from his tightly clasped hand with two straws protruding to his face. "You're serious?"

He nodded, thrusting his hand out for her to pick a straw. "Come on. It's a fifty–fifty chance. Surely you take risks."

Yes, she took risks. The biggest one was getting involved with Sloan in the first place. She was betting her future happiness on the outcome.

Her hand hovered over a straw. Then suddenly she decided to pick the other one. The short straw!

"Now, the next time I come down here I want you to cook me a meal."

Her heart fluttered, but she managed to retort lightly, "Are you a male chauvinist, Sloan Hunter?"

He laughed, the sound wonderful to her ears. "If I had been left with the short straw, you would have demanded the same thing. Are you a female chauvinist, Kendall Spencer?"

The popping sound of the toaster saved Kendall from having to answer. She retrieved the two burned pieces of bread and held them up. "I'm not responsible for this minor disaster."

"That toaster has been on and off the whole vacation. Put two more pieces in. Maybe this time it will work."

By the time they sat down at the kitchen table to eat, they had managed to prepare an edible breakfast. "Maybe if we work hard enough at it, we can be a team. Of course, we used most of the food in the cabin to arrive at this," Kendall commented.

A serious expression touched Sloan's features. "We *are* a team, Kendall," he said vehemently.

The sound of the hatchback slamming shut jolted Kendall, bombarding her with a dismal finality. Sloan had locked up the cabin and it already looked deserted, as though no one had lived in it for a long time. His luggage was in his car and all that was left was a simple good-bye.

As Sloan made one final check that everything was securely locked, Kendall turned away from the cabin and struggled to swallow the lump lodged in her throat. The palms of her hands felt clammy, and she kept wiping them on her jeans, but the icy feeling wouldn't go away. *Will this numb, almost dead feeling ever change? Will time heal it? Will it ever get any easier to watch him leave?* Somehow she doubted it would.

All her firm resolution not to cry evaporated now that the moment was upon her. Their time together hadn't been long enough. She wanted to cling to him, to plead with him to stay, at least for another night. But she wouldn't, couldn't, because this scene was just as hard for him as for her.

Finally she managed some control over her floundering emotions, enough to turn back. She gasped. He was standing only a few feet from her, staring at her with a raw look in his eyes that wrenched her heart, slowing its beating down to a throb.

"Kendall, I . . ." His voice failed him and he visibly swallowed. Clearing his throat, he tried again. "Kendall, I'll call you tomorrow evening."

"I won't be home until after eight. I have a meeting in Little Rock." So polite, so formal sounding, Kendall thought with dismay.

"I . . . Dammit, Kendall!" He closed the gap between them and pulled her into his arms. "I love you, darling. Please don't forget that during the following weeks. They're going to be tough for both of us to get through. You have my number and if you ever need to talk, call me at home or work, regardless of the time.''

''I will.'' The words came out in a low whisper because her throat had tightened again, and this time she couldn't stop the tears from welling in her eyes and rolling down her cheeks.

Placing a finger under her chin, Sloan lifted it, his eyes shimmering. He bent and kissed her tear-streaked cheeks, the action producing more tears.

Fiercely Kendall wiped at her face. ''Oh, Sloan, I didn't want to cry . . . to cause a scene. What a way to send you off.''

Cradling her head tenderly within his hands, he looked deeply into her eyes. ''It won't be forever, darling. We'll talk every day if you want.''

''The telephone company will love us.''

''Hell, what's money for except to spend on things that make us happy? And believe me, to hear your voice would make me happy.''

Kendall ran her hands over his chest as though she were a sculptor creating a work of art. ''Are you sure you'll be all right? You didn't get much sleep last night.''

He smiled. ''If it will make you feel any better, I'll call you when I arrive in St. Louis if you don't mind being awakened at one or two in the morning.''

''I don't think I'll be asleep, and yes, I would like that.'' She caught a glimpse of the time on her wristwatch. ''I guess you'd better be going. It's already past five, Sloan,'' she added reluctantly.

"I don't think I'll ever like five o'clock again," he said in dead seriousness.

"Good-bye, Sloan."

"No. No good-byes. Just until I see you again."

His arms tensed about her and his mouth lowered to sample the delights of hers. She parted her lips gladly to allow him access to the soft interior of her mouth. The kiss expanded as they both clung desperately to the other. It would have to last them a long time and they were reluctant to end it.

Finally, when Kendall thought there was no more air left in her lungs, she drew away. After dragging several deep breaths into her, she whispered, "I love you, Sloan. Please drive carefully."

Without another word, Sloan turned away from her and strode to the car. He glanced at her once more before putting his car into Drive and heading out toward the highway that would take him away from her.

Now she wanted to cry, but the tears wouldn't come. She needed the emotional release, but, instead, all the pain she felt was bottled up inside of her, eating away at her heart. She stood on the dirt road in front of the cabin for a long time, staring at the place where she had last seen Sloan's car. Chilled in the ninety-degree weather, Kendall rubbed her hands up and down her arms, but it did nothing to melt the icy wall that encased her heart.

The distant sound of a motorboat finally roused her from her trancelike state, and she quickly walked to her car, not looking back at the cabin or lake. In the driver's seat, she rested her head on the cold metal of the steering wheel, shutting her eyes for a moment as she assembled her composure enough to drive.

On the highway she headed the car toward the cove where they had first made love, as though she were a criminal returning to the scene of the crime. Parking under a grove of pine trees, Kendall walked toward the lakeshore. With each step she took toward the spot where they had lain, her heart felt as if it were expanding, threatening to choke off her next breath.

She wasn't even halfway to the lakeside when she whirled around and ran up the slight incline toward her car. It hurt too much to be there, or, for that matter, at the cabin. She didn't think she would ever be able to visit either one without Sloan again.

For the next hour Kendall drove around, going nowhere in particular. Scenes of her and Sloan over the past five weeks paraded through her thoughts. In her mind she relived their meeting, their first kiss and the night of the arts-and-crafts fair. When she had finished replaying their time together, her mind felt emptied, her body exhausted, as though she had been on a treadmill for hours.

Finally as the sun was setting, Kendall directed her car toward her house, feeling the need now to talk with her grandmother. Suddenly she didn't want to be alone. Forcing her mind away from thoughts of Sloan, she concentrated only on the ribbon of road in front of her. Pulling into her driveway, she switched off the engine and looked toward the house. No lights. Strange. It was dark and usually her grandmother had a light on in the living room by that time.

When Kendall unlocked the front door and stepped into the house, an eerie quiet assailed her. She scanned the living room, afraid to take another step into the house. Something was wrong! She could feel it in the very marrow of her bones. As though someone had snapped his fingers and brought her out of a deep hypnotic spell, she moved quickly forward, walking through every room, her anxiety intensifying.

At last, she went outside to her grandmother's workshed; a bright light was shining in the small window. It was too quiet! Placing her hand on the doorknob, she hesitated, frightened she would find her grandmother unconscious on the floor. Galvanized into action with that thought, she thrust open the door and advanced into the empty room.

Relieved, Kendall sagged against a worktable, having decided she was allowing her imagination to run away with her. But taking one last glance around the room, she noticed that some tools were missing. Her grandmother was a neat person, but the shed was too clean. She inspected the room closely, her attention caught by a sheet of paper, propped up on a worktable.

Her name leaped off the white paper. Kendall's gaze flashed to the signature at the bottom of the note. Her grandmother's.

Paralyzed, Kendall made no move to pick up the piece of paper. Somehow she knew what the note from her grandmother said. Maria Spencer had left for Arizona without saying good-bye. She had told Missi the night of Sloan's birthday party that she hated good-byes, but Kendall had never thought her grandmother wouldn't tell her when she was leaving. Had she been so wrapped up in Sloan these past few days that she had neglected the signs, or had not taken the time to talk with her grandmother about her specific plans? A few weeks before Maria had said she would be leaving soon, but Kendall hadn't imagined that it would be this soon. Not when she needed to talk with her grandmother! Not when she needed a loved one to help her through the next few days!

With a trembling hand, Kendall finally reached for the letter, reading it out loud:

"Anna called Saturday morning and told me everything was set for me to come. So I decided to leave today. Flora drove me to the airport in Little Rock. I know you needed the time to be with Sloan. I waited as long as I could, then decided that it was best you hadn't returned by the time I needed to leave.

"Kendall, if you love the man, follow your heart. I never regretted leaving my people to marry your grandfather. Now, though, it's time for me to return to where I was born. I will write when I'm settled. Please understand, my child.

                          With all my love,
                               Grandma"

The paper slipped from Kendall's fingers and floated to the floor. She wished she could follow her heart, but she couldn't leave the people of Spencerville without a doctor. She was too disciplined and dedicated to turn her back on them, just as Sloan was with his work at the research laboratory.

With leadened steps, Kendall retraced her path back to the house and collapsed onto the couch, the room bathed in the shadows of night. If only she had come straight home after seeing Sloan off, maybe she would have made it in time to see her grandmother. She should have been the one to have driven Maria to the airport. She had let her grandmother down again. Hugging a soft pillow to her, Kendall stared out a window at the blackness beyond, her life fragmented, completely changed in five short weeks.

She didn't know how long she sat there in the dark, but the jarring ring of the phone split the air, bringing Kendall to her feet.

"Hello, Dr. Spencer speaking." Her voice sounded strained, as though it hadn't been used for a while.

"Kendall, are you all right?" Sloan's voice was marked with a deep concern.

No! I hurt all over. I want you here with me, not in St. Louis. I'm all alone, Sloan! Don't you understand! There's no one left in Spencerville. Words she wanted to say constricted her heart as her grip on the phone tightened.

"Kendall!"

"I'm sorry, Sloan. I was just surprised you were calling so soon. You can't be in St. Louis already." Kendall switched on a lamp and turned to glance at the wall clock. One o'clock!

"I don't drive *that much* over the speed limit. Yes,

I'm in St. Louis sitting at my desk in my den talking to a beautiful, desirous woman. Did I wake you?''

"No. I . . ." Kendall paused, not sure what to say into a cold machine when she wanted to be talking with Sloan face to face.

"Something is wrong, Kendall. I can feel it."

"Grandma left for Arizona today."

"Oh, no, Kendall, I'm sorry. That must have been a very rough scene saying good-bye to her right after me."

An indescribable tenderness touched her. She felt as if a steel chain had been pulled tighter about her chest and she was fighting for each breath. It was killing her to listen to him being so wonderful and understanding. And yet he was too far away to hold, to caress. She wanted to hang up the phone, only she wouldn't break her link with him.

"I didn't see her before she left. I stayed at the cabin, then drove around. She was gone by the time I got back home. If I had known she was leaving, I . . ." She halted. What would she have done? Left Sloan earlier? Made Sloan stop by the house? Pleaded with her grandmother to wait another day? She didn't like any of the alternatives.

"Kendall, I wish I was there." His voice was pitched to a low, husky level. "You're hurting, darling. I want to be there to comfort you, to . . . Dammit! I'm hurting. I want you to comfort me."

This was doing neither one of them any good, Kendall realized. What were the ground rules of a relationship that had to be conducted over long distance? They were tearing each other apart with wishes that they knew wouldn't come true.

In a much steadier voice, Kendall continued. "Sloan, it's okay. You said the next few weeks would be hard and we're just finding out how hard. Will you call me tomorrow night? We'll talk then when we aren't so tired. Besides, I wouldn't want the research chief to fall asleep at his first staff meeting in two months."

He chuckled, a warm liquid sound. "They would never let me live it down. I'll speak with you at nine tomorrow night."

"I'll be here waiting by the phone."

When Kendall hung up, her fingers tenderly grazed the receiver. She had never particularly liked telephones, but this small instrument would be her bond with Sloan in the future.

Chapter Ten

*Y*ou can! I'm going to see you next weekend!'' Kendall exclaimed, cradling the phone to her ear and snuggling deeper under the sheets to enjoy her conversation with Sloan. They were talking later than usual because he had had a dinner engagement with the president of the university.

"You heard me, lady. It's been five, long miserable weeks, but I finally think I've managed to work in a few free days and you're the first person I thought of spending them with.''

"I'd better have been,'' Kendall retorted in mock sternness. "When will you fly down?''

"I should be there about eight if my colleagues don't come up with something else to go wrong. Losing that funding sure hurt the project.''

The previous week they had talked for an hour about the Franklin Foundation pulling its money out of the project because it had run into some financial problems of its own. At first Sloan had been angry, but by the time they had hung up, he had calmed down and had already planned on where he was going to get the funding. It wouldn't be easy with the economy so tight, but if anyone could, Kendall felt sure it would be Sloan.

"Let's see. That means I'll be with you in four days, twenty-one hours."

"And not one hour later," Sloan said, caressing her with his voice. "You know, before I used to look forward to spending a lot of time at the lab. Now, though, I'm beginning to resent it because it's keeping me from you. Taking a six-week vacation sure can screw things up."

"If you hadn't taken a six-week vacation, you wouldn't have met me. Besides, you know you don't mean it about your work. Oh, I almost forgot. I got a letter from my grandmother today."

"How's she doing?"

Frowning, Kendall was glad Sloan couldn't see her face at the moment. "She's okay. At least that's what she tells me. I wish I could talk to her on the phone. You know she's been writing Missi every week." Kendall paused, wondering if she should tell Sloan everything and add to his worries.

"Okay, Doc, what are you keeping from me?"

"Grandma says Missi isn't very happy, Sloan. Apparently she's beginning to have even more asthma episodes

than before. Sandra won't let her go swimming with the
other kids or go to camp, and Missi isn't taking that very
well.''

"I know. Sandra blames it all on me for allowing
Missi to do those things in Arkansas. What's so damned
frustrating is that there isn't much I can do here in St.
Louis about Missi's situation. Do you know that Ted has
even tried to talk to Sandra about letting Missi do more
activities? She just won't listen.''

Sadness edged his voice, deepening Kendall's frown.

"But I'm glad she has your grandmother. They have a
bond that's special.''

"Sloan, I love you," Kendall said vehemently, as if
that would soothe the sadness.

"I wish I was there with you—in bed.''

The seductive tone of his voice sent her heart slamming against her breast. "How did you know I was in
bed?''

Laughing softly, he answered, "Just a lucky guess.
Good night, love. Thank God, I'll see you at the end of
the week.''

"Kendall, I can't come." Defeat, mixed with exhaustion, punctuated Sloan's words.

"What's wrong?" Her panic increased with her question.

"Missi ran away this afternoon and I'm flying
to Atlanta in an hour. Even if she's found, and I pray
she is, I'll have to work through the weekend to catch
up.''

"Is there anything I can do?" Kendall was very

worried about Missi and at the same time disappointed that she wouldn't be seeing Sloan.

"No. Damn, Kendall, I should have seen this coming. All the warning signs were there, but I was so wrapped up in trying to get the money my project needs and in clearing away enough time to fly down to see you that I ignored them."

"Don't blame yourself for the situation, Sloan. It won't do any good for Missi or you."

"I've got to go, Kendall, or I'll miss my plane. I'll call you when we find her."

He didn't have to say "if we find her." She heard the worry, the doubt in his voice.

"She's okay?" was the first thing Kendall asked when she heard Sloan's voice.

"Yes, thank God. It's been hell these last thirty-six hours. The only good thing that has come out of all this is that Sandra is willing to listen to Ted and me now. I wish I could say she was going to do everything I wanted, but at least now she sees how truly unhappy Missi is. I know Sandra won't completely change her overprotective ways, but maybe with some help she'll temper them."

"I'm glad, Sloan." Kendall sat behind her desk in her office, shifting the phone to her other ear. "Sloan, I think I can arrange to take three days off two weeks from now."

"In two weeks?"

"Yes, Mrs. Carter should have delivered by then and Dr. Hatfield will cover for me."

"Fine," Sloan said, his words forced.

"Are you sure, Sloan?"

"Yes, Doc. I want to see you more than anything. I'm flying back to St. Louis tomorrow afternoon. I'll call you tomorrow evening the usual time. Then we can talk more."

"Give a hug to Missi for me."

After saying good-bye to Sloan, Kendall sat behind her desk, drumming her fingers on it. She had received mixed vibrations from Sloan. Were his feelings for her changing? Or was it merely that he was mentally and physically exhausted, which made him sound different, more distant on the phone? All of a sudden she was afraid to go to St. Louis and discover the past weeks' fantasies of their next meeting were all wrong.

The "Fasten Seat Belt" sign flashed on and Kendall automatically checked to see if hers still was. In ten minutes she would be in Sloan's arms, kissing him. For two weeks she hadn't allowed herself to get excited about the trip to St. Louis because she was afraid something would come up to ruin it. Until she had stepped onto the plane in Little Rock, she had half waited for the phone to ring with an emergency or Sloan telling her not to come, that something had come up at the lab and he had to work all weekend. Each time the phone had rung, she had found herself holding her breath and not answering until the fifth or sixth ring, her hands trembling.

She needed this weekend badly, Kendall decided as

she stood to exit the plane. It wasn't that her love for Sloan was weakening. It was just that she needed to be reassured by him in a way the phone could never convey. They hadn't known each other that long, and distance didn't always make the heart grow fonder.

Walking into the airport terminal, Kendall eagerly searched the mass of people waiting by the gate for passengers. But as the crowd began to thin, people pairing off and leaving, Kendall's excitement diminished. Her plane had been fifteen minutes late, and yet there was no sign of Sloan anywhere.

So much for her plan to run into his outstretched arms, she thought, and moved to sit in the gate area and wait. A young man jogging toward her caught her attention and she paused.

A half-grin, full of a silent apology, spread across the young man's face as he stopped in front of her. "Dr. Spencer?"

"Yes?"

The young man extended his hand. "I'm Andy Miller. I work with Dr. Hunter. He got tied up at the lab and asked me to pick you up and take you to his house."

Kendall shook the man's hand, trying to smile, but not succeeding. "How long will he be?"

"I'm not sure, ma'am. The people from the Matrix Institute showed up unexpectedly and he's with them now."

After picking up her piece of luggage, they walked to the parking lot, where Kendall got into an old, beat-up Ford for the ride to Sloan's. She couldn't shake the feeling of dread as they neared his house. The weekend was starting out badly. She had built this first meeting up in her mind; she had imagined Sloan sweeping her off her feet and not setting her down until Sunday evening, when she had to return to Spencerville. Instead, both of her feet were firmly planted on the ground.

When Andy Miller dropped her off at Sloan's, Kendall felt a frustrating letdown that he hadn't even been able to meet her at his house. She was left alone to explore Sloan's two-story house, which was as empty as her heart. Her anger began to simmer at each passing minute.

Normally she would have appreciated the beauty of Sloan's home, decorated in an understated elegance that indicated another facet of his personality she hadn't glimpsed. But after an hour of wandering from room to room, brewing herself a cup of tea and drinking it, her anger began to boil.

At seven o'clock, three hours after she had landed at the airport, Kendall was sitting in Sloan's living room with her arms folded across her breasts and her foot impatiently tapping the carpeted floor. When she heard the front door open, her frown strengthened. Sloan halted in the doorway to the living room, his welcoming smile dying on his lips.

"It couldn't be helped, Kendall," Sloan said, his expression bland, his body tensing as though he were instantly preparing himself for battle.

"I've been sitting here for two and a half hours wondering if you would even be showing up or if I would receive one of your telephone calls telling me you couldn't make it.'' Sarcasm ate into her words like acid.

His own mounting anger was expressed in the rigid set of his shoulders, the grim line of his mouth. "Kendall, you know I've been having trouble with the project lately. I can't just abandon it, not when the institute that might give us the money we need comes into town. I was afraid they might show up this weekend, but I didn't want to tell you not to come in case they didn't.''

Her anger started melting as she felt the urge to be held by him. Her stiff body went limp and she sagged back against the couch. Sloan crossed the room and sat down next to her, but he didn't attempt to take her into his arms or to even touch her.

Sloan flicked her a glance, and a rueful grin. "Did we just have our first fight, Doc?''

"I'd say more like our first misunderstanding. I'm sorry, Sloan. For a while I let my expectations get in the way of my understanding and logic. I know it hasn't been easy for you, and I certainly don't want to add to your problems.'' Kendall twisted about to look Sloan straight in the eye. "But, Sloan, out of the last eight weeks all we will have is the next few days. Don't you think we both deserve these days for ourselves? Believe it or not, I think things will survive without us for forty-eight hours. I want you, Sloan.''

His quick intake of breath charged the atmosphere. Expelling a heavy sigh, he leaned back, looking away from her. "I'd be the first to agree with you, but I'm afraid things don't always work out the way we want.''

He hesitated, a conflict raging inside him. Then, as though to fortify himself for what he was going to say, his expression became unreadable. "We have to go to a faculty barbecue tonight and there is no way I can get out of it. I still haven't convinced all the people of Matrix Institute to give us the money, and they are leaving tomorrow morning." Turning to face her, he seized her hand and brought it to his lips. "We'll stay at the party only as long as necessary, Kendall, but I must go. I know you want to be alone, and so do I." He kissed each fingertip, sending a bolt of sensations darting up her arm. "I've dreamed of this weekend, too, darling, and the things I have in mind for us would be best done in private."

She wanted to shout, "For just this one weekend why can't you say the hell with your work!" She had the strong urge to pull away from him and demand he make a choice, at least for the next few days—her, or his work. She couldn't disregard the feeling that she needed to be first in his life above all else.

"All I'm asking for is the weekend, Sloan," she murmured, stopping the progression of his mouth over her wrist.

"And you'll have it after tonight." He surrendered his hold on her hand and it fell back to her side. "Don't you think when the committee from Matrix walked through my door thirty minutes before I was to leave to pick you up that I wanted to tell them, 'Sorry, I already have plans which don't include you'?" With a jerky movement, Sloan rubbed his jaw. "I wanted to so much, but I couldn't. Just as you could never turn your back on your work. We are two of a kind. Our dedication to our work is a big part of us.''

All the anger was drained from Kendall. What he said was true. But the most important fact was that she really had no right to make demands on him as she had. They had made no commitment to each other beyond this weekend.

''What should I wear? And when do we have to leave?'' Kendall spoke the questions in a monotone, defeat evident in her words.

Sloan gently clasped her head between his hands and stared down at her tenderly. ''Oh, Kendall, I know what you're thinking. You are very important to me, as I hope I am to you. Please believe that, darling.''

''I'm trying, Sloan. One part of me hears clearly what you say. But there's another part of me that needs constant reassurance because our relationship is fragile. Not seeing a man but every few months can do that to a woman.'' A smile, full of self-mockery, touched her mouth as her hand came up to cover his.

''There is no doubt in my mind that I love you, Doc.'' Kendall turned her face to kiss the palm of his hand. ''When do we have to be there?'' There was a husky appeal in the question, all her needs and wants honing into one sharp, intense point of desire in her body.

''Right now, I'm afraid, but I think we're going to develop car trouble that will make us at least an hour late.'' Sloan rose and held his hand out for her. ''Have you seen my bedroom? I have an interesting oil painting of a lake I'd like to show you.''

''Why, Sloan Hunter, that's the oldest line in the

book,'' Kendall quipped as she moved toward the stairs, nestled within his embrace.

Kendall guessed somewhere in the back of her mind she had thought there was the possibility that Sloan would move to Arkansas to be with her, maybe working in Little Rock and commuting to Spencerville. But after spending the weekend with him she knew in her heart that would never happen.

She had seen firsthand the importance of his work at the research laboratory when he had had to go to the university Saturday morning for a last-minute conference with the Matrix representatives. She had accompanied him and waited for an hour in his office while they had finalized the funding agreement. Afterward, he had given her the grand tour of the facilities and she had seen the zealous look in his eyes when he had explained to her the various parts of the project.

Later she had discovered one of the reasons for Sloan's fervent dedication to the project. His father had died from lung cancer five years before. Sloan had told her Saturday evening about his childhood and about how he had had to watch his father die slowly from the cancer that had been eating away at him.

Kendall knew of the anguish that Sloan had felt while waiting helplessly for the inevitable. She had witnessed it enough as a doctor. At least her own father's death had been mercifully quick.

She had gone to Sloan, who was standing by the fireplace, and offered herself to him, wanting to ease the painful memory from his mind, at least for a short time.

That night they had made desperate love, as though they couldn't get enough of each other.

Now, it was time for her to leave. She placed her last garment in her suitcase and shut it with a click. She scanned Sloan's bedroom once more to make sure she hadn't left anything behind. Not for the first time, the feeling of not belonging there besieged Kendall. Sloan's house was beautiful, neat and elegant. Not like her house, where there was a lived-in atmosphere, homey and cozy with sturdy furniture that was made for comfort. There had been times when they had been sitting in his living room surrounded by glass figurines and silk-covered furniture that Kendall had been afraid to relax.

Kendall's survey of the bedroom stopped at the door to the bathroom, where Sloan was standing, a towel knotted at his waist, his hair damp from the shower he had taken.

"I'm sure going to miss you, Doc. You make this house seem like a home again."

Kendall's gray eyes widened. "This isn't you, is it?" she asked, waving her hand.

"Doc, does this look like me?" He, too, gestured broadly with a wide sweep of his arm.

"Frankly, no."

Sloan advanced into the room and walked toward his closet, dropping his towel after selecting a pair of jeans and a blue-and-cream-striped shirt to wear. Kendall's gaze traveled hungrily over his trim body.

"Sandra decorated this house, but when she left, she didn't want to take anything of our marriage into her new one. So I was left with all this and I just haven't had the time to do anything to change the house. I'm usually not here much anyway." Sloan stepped into his jeans, turning to face her while shrugging into his shirt.

Kendall stood very still, watching his every movement as he buttoned his shirt. Her heart felt as if each beat were a great effort and that at any moment it would give up. She shut her eyes for a few seconds, and when she opened them again, Sloan was staring at her intensely.

"When will I see you again?" Kendall asked, her voice quavering.

"I don't know, Kendall. I'm going to be very busy for the next month or so. We're starting another phase of the project which will require a lot of extra time."

Somewhere in her mind Kendall felt a door close, something begin to change, as though she were a caterpillar starting to weave its cocoon to begin another stage of its life. Everything inside of her was coiled into a tight ball.

Muttering an oath under his breath, Sloan crossed the short space that separated them and clasped her upper arms in a bruising grip. "Kendall, don't look at me like that. I want you so badly it hurts. Somehow things are going to work out for us."

"How? When?" Her voice cracked, her gaze dropping to the first button of his shirt. She couldn't look into his eyes any longer. They reflected all the churning emotions she was feeling.

"I don't know for sure how or when. But I have to believe it will." The grip on her arms loosened, and he slid his hands up to her shoulders, then around to pull her close to him. "I agree with your grandmother. Good-byes are horrible."

She drew back slightly. "Well, Sloan Hunter, don't think you're going to get away with not taking me to the airport and saying good-bye."

He didn't say anything. Instead, he touched her lips in a caressing kiss, rubbing his mouth against hers in a sensual movement. "Maybe there's a later flight, Doc. I don't want to say good-bye just yet."

"No, Sloan. I have the last flight out and I have to be back tomorrow morning." She lifted her hand to stroke the nape of his neck, running her fingers through the hair in the back.

He sighed. "Somehow I knew you were going to say that. Well, then this kiss will have to last us a long time."

Sloan closed his lips over hers, seeking the softness within her mouth, their tongues touching and withdrawing, then touching again. As the kiss lengthened and deepened, Kendall became attuned entirely to Sloan, the scent of soap and his after-shave lotion mingling with her fragrance to form a myriad of tantalizing smells.

But as the kiss ended, Kendall felt that door locking shut and she was trapped in a small room with no way out. As they parted to finish getting ready to leave for the airport, she searched frantically in her mind for the door but it had vanished. The small cubicle she felt imprisoned in was four bleak walls with no windows or doors. She shuddered as she thought of the future.

Chapter Eleven

The room seemed to be shrinking as she struggled to make it through each day, waiting eagerly by the phone at the usual time that Sloan called. But as the weeks passed and they couldn't manage to see each other, her doubts grew and intensified.

It was midnight and Kendall had talked with Sloan three hours before. She had tried to sleep but she couldn't. Pacing back and forth in her bedroom, Kendall had reached a decision. Their relationship couldn't continue as it was. She had to have more than phone calls and a few days every couple of months.

Every time she talked with Sloan it was becoming harder and harder for her to hang up and to go on with her life as though everything was all right. It wasn't! Their conversations were becoming strained, a subtle tension in their voices.

When he called the following night, she would tell him it was over between them. She had to get on with her life and find some kind of happiness. Maybe in time the memories of Sloan would fade and she could find someone else to love.

"Who are you trying to fool?" she asked herself aloud as she sank onto her bed, her legs weak, her hands quivering. There would be only one man like Sloan in her life. But then he wasn't really in her life, only on the fringes. She wanted more from a relationship.

In the months since Sloan had left, she had stepped up her search for another doctor but hadn't had any luck. Not even one doctor had inquired about Spencerville in the last six weeks and only two since she had started looking.

Kendall lay on the bed and stared at the ceiling. Logically she knew she would have a difficult time finding someone to practice in Spencerville. There was no way she could leave unless she did, and even then it would be hard for her to move. She was emotionally tied to the townspeople. Logically she knew she should be patient, that someday things would work out as Sloan believed, but emotionally she couldn't take any more of this. She felt as if she were being ripped in two, and as the days turned into weeks without seeing Sloan, the hurt twisted even deeper.

The only way to handle the situation was to sever her ties completely with him. Closing her eyes, Kendall lifted her hand to massage her temple, her head pounding from the last few hours of contemplation. She had a strong impulse before she lost her courage to call Sloan right away.

Kendall bolted upright in bed at the sound of the phone ringing. She hurriedly answered it. The only calls she received at this time of night were emergencies.

"Kendall Spencer?"

"Speaking."

"This is Anna."

Kendall clenched the phone painfully. Something was wrong with her grandmother. She felt it deep within.

"I'm sorry to be calling you at this time, but Maria died about two hours ago."

The hammering against her brow increased until Kendall thought her head would explode. "No! It's not fair!" she wanted to shout. But instead she asked, "How?"

"I found her in her bedroom at her desk right before I was going to bed. I had noticed she had been more tired lately, but that was all. I don't think she suffered."

"I'll be there as soon as I can," Kendall said, finding out the directions to the Indian village, then hanging up.

For a long time Kendall sat on her bed, her hand still on the phone, staring at the floor. She tried to inhale deep breaths, but she felt as though she were suffocating. Picking up the receiver again, she started to call Sloan but slammed the phone down before punching the last number. No, she had to start somewhere, not depending on Sloan for support. Determinedly she looked up the number of an airline, then lifted the receiver to her ear. She would face this alone.

*   *   *

Kendall sat on the twin bed that her grandmother had slept in, her gaze absently scanning the small room, the only other furniture being a four-drawer chest and a chair and table that served as a desk. The funeral would be in an hour and she couldn't bring herself to dress.

Combing her fingers repeatedly through her tangled hair trying to make it smooth, Kendall shivered from the cold, the early morning chill still clinging to the four-room house. She pulled her robe tighter about her and hugged her arms to her.

When she had arrived the day before, it had been very difficult for her to adjust to the poverty in the village where her grandmother had been living. Then Kendall had discovered that there wasn't a doctor in the area and that her grandmother hadn't seen one and she felt guilty that she hadn't been there for her grandmother. If she had, maybe she would have seen the warning signs of her grandmother's heart attack and been able to prevent her from dying.

The land around the village was beautiful, with the tall mountains in the background and vast stretches of desert. The proud villagers were her grandmother's people, the land her heritage, and Kendall was beginning to understand the lure the land had held for her grandmother.

The previous night she had walked with Anna and stood on a bluff looking down on the desert floor below. Long after her cousin had returned to the village, Kendall had stayed, thinking, trying to sort out the mess her life was in. No satisfying answers came to mind, but the balm of nature had calmed her and made it easier for her to join the villagers at Anna's house.

Kendall's head snapped up at the sound of the door creaking open. Her eyes widened, then filled with tears that she had kept in check ever since she had heard about her grandmother's death.

"Sloan," she whispered, her mind grasping and clinging to the fact that he was standing in front of her, only a few feet away and that she could reach out and touch him.

"I couldn't let you go through this without me, Kendall." He was beside her on the bed in seconds, taking her into the warmth of his embrace and stroking her back with soothing movements.

"How?" she murmured against his shirt, her arms slipping around to clasp him.

"Missi. She called me yesterday afternoon to tell me that Maria had died. Your cousin called her. Maria had been writing Missi a letter when she died and your cousin felt she should know." Sloan paused for a moment. "Why did I have to hear it from Missi?" he asked.

Kendall winced at the pained tone in his voice. She had hurt him, but at the moment she didn't see how they wouldn't end up hurting each other badly. "You've been so busy lately that I didn't think you could come."

The back of his hand caressed her cheek. "So you thought you'd face this alone." A slow smile altered the intense look on his face. "I love you, Kendall, and no project in the world would keep me away if you needed me."

Kendall wanted to smile, but she felt so numb inside. In the past four months her life had changed drastically and for the first time in her life she was having a difficult time dealing with the changes. Before there had never been any question about what she would do with her life. Before it had always been so organized, so mapped out for her that she had given little thought to her future.

"Kendall?" Sloan's voice was full of concern as he compelled her to look at him by placing a finger under her chin and forcing her head around.

This time Kendall did smile. Sloan had come when she had needed him and had been too stubborn to ask. "How did you find this place?"

Laughter rumbled from deep in his chest. "That, Doc, wasn't an easy feat. All I can say after traveling over that dirt road is that I'm glad I rented a Jeep in Flagstaff." He kissed the tip of her nose, continuing: "I arrived late last night and had to wait till this morning. That was one of the longest, loneliest nights I've spent, knowing the pain you were feeling over your grandmother's death. You weren't very far away from me, but I knew I wouldn't find this village in the dark, so I waited, tossing and turning the whole night."

"Grandma's funeral is very soon. I'd better get dressed. I look a mess. I did my share of tossing and turning last night, too."

"You look beautiful. I wish I could see you like this

more often, your hair tousled from sleep, your eyes languid, your lips . . ."—he leaned forward and covered her mouth with his, his tongue tasting of her—". . . waiting to be kissed." He whispered against them, then sought to deepen the kiss again with a fiery impatience.

When they broke apart, Kendall knew she wouldn't say anything to Sloan about ending their relationship. Seeing him again, she realized that he was too important to her and that she would just have to make the best of their impossible situation.

Grinning down at her, he brushed his fingers through her tangles, saying, "I guess I'd better let you get dressed. You want me to wait in the other room?"

"No. We have so little time together, Sloan, that I hate to be away from you even for a few minutes. Please stay."

His hand slid to the nape of her neck and he dragged her toward him, his lips claiming hers. "You don't have to twist my arm, Doc, on that one," he muttered.

If he hàdn't been holding her head, the force of his kiss would have driven Kendall backward. The hunger in them was unquenchable as their tongues parried, their bodies dissolving against one another.

"After your grandmother's funeral, Kendall, I want to take you away for a couple of days."

"I should get back to Spencerville. I left so unexpectedly."

"I know we both should do a lot of things, but you also need some time away, just for yourself. Your grandmother was very special to you and I have a feeling if you went right back to Spencerville you would never fully face her death. If you don't want me with you, I'll understand.''

Her brow furrowed. ''Don't want you with me? When my mother died I was too young to understand what had happened. When my father died two years ago, my grandmother was there and we leaned on each other. I see more death than most people, but, Sloan, I'm not sure I've really come to terms with it. I had to throw myself into my work right after my father died because there was a whole town full of people who depended on me to keep them healthy. I never mourned for my father because I didn't have the time.'' Kendall stood, walked to the window and stared out onto the village plaza. ''Now, I have no more immediate family left and I feel so empty inside. I feel as if my emotions have frozen.'' She turned and faced Sloan, who still sat on the bed. ''Hold me, Sloan. Hold me.''

In two quick strides, Sloan was in front of her, drawing her to him.

''I'm scared, Sloan. I've never felt so alone as when Anna called and told me my grandmother had died. All of a sudden it hit me. You in St. Louis. My father and grandmother dead.'' Tears welled in her gray eyes and spilled onto her cheeks. ''I realized I'd never see them again, and yet all I felt was nothing inside. Nothing!''

''I'm here. You're not alone, Kendall. Only miles separate us.''

The tears Kendall had wanted to cry two days before

continued to cascade down her face, soaking Sloan's shirt as he held her tightly against him, rubbing her back and telling her over and over that he loved her.

Kendall leaned against the railing and peered over into the Grand Canyon, breathing deeply of the cool fall air. Even in the dim light of dawn she could glimpse the Colorado River winding its way through the canyon.

Two hands grasped her arms from behind and hauled her back against a solid body. "I got up at an ungodly hour to watch the sun rise only because you were so disappointed that we had arrived after the sun had set last night. The least you could do, woman, is keep me warm." Sloan snuggled closer, his arms crossed over her breasts, his breath touching her neck with a caressing heat.

"You know you wanted to see the sunrise as much as I did," Kendall scolded him gently, burrowing closer into the warmth of his body. "I guess, though, we should have come prepared for colder weather. But then I didn't know I would be visiting the Grand Canyon yesterday morning. And when I left Spencerville, I wasn't thinking of snow in the middle of October."

"I couldn't have let you come to Arizona and not see the canyon. Isn't it breathtaking?"

"Yes," Kendall murmured as she gazed down into the valley far below, then at the play of light on the serrated walls of sheer rock. An early morning fog lingered in some places, a reddish tint, reflecting the sun's light. It was serenely quiet. If the railing hadn't been there, Kendall would have thought they had stepped back in time to when the Spaniards had first seen the Grand Canyon. Forests of pine trees surrounded them in the background and she could imagine the Spaniards' stunned surprise at finding this hole in the ground blocking their way.

"What would you like to do today, Doc?" Sloan whispered into her ear before nipping lightly on its shell.

She turned within his embrace, her hands lacing together behind his neck. "Walk, talk, sleep, be with you." There was an urgency in her voice because they had only one full day before they had to part to return to their separate homes. One day! And how long would that have to last her?

"Well, how about, let's walk to our car, talk while we eat breakfast and catch up on our sleep afterward?" A devilishly lazy gleam flared in his eyes.

"Thank you, Sloan, for being there for me last night. Thank you for listening. I needed to talk about my grandmother, to put her memories in perspective, and you helped me by holding me and letting me just ramble on and on when I know you were tired."

"I will always be there to listen, Kendall." All playfulness fled his expression.

But Kendall couldn't help but wonder if he would as they drove toward the El Tovar, a lodge where they were staying on the south rim. There was an underlying desperation to this time together that Kendall felt and couldn't shake. Maybe it was because her grandmother had died and had been buried the day before, but somehow she didn't think so. In her mind she kept thinking this was the beginning of the end.

When they arrived at the El Tovar, a majestic hotel built at century's turn with Douglas fir logs hauled all the way from Oregon, Sloan and Kendall paused again to view the canyon below them. The sun was up, painting the cliffs a golden red. The noises of a new day drifted to them, underscoring a return to reality that for a while Kendall had escaped at the lookout.

As Kendall watched a group of hikers preparing for their journey into the valley, Sloan slipped his arm around her waist. "I didn't bring my hiking shoes. But we could always ride a mule into the canyon."

Kendall shook her head. "I've heard stories of the narrow paths to the floor. I think I'll stay up here. Besides"—she tried to stifle a yawn—"I'm sleepy. I think everything is finally catching up with me."

"I'm glad that isn't a comment on my company," Sloan said with a laugh as he guided her toward the sprawling front porch of the El Tovar.

Inside the dining room they were seated at a table set off in the corner. After ordering a big breakfast, Kendall sat back in her chair to enjoy the atmosphere of relaxed gentility. The walls made of logs, the Indian paintings and the huge fireplace added to the quiet elegance from years past.

"Are you all right today?" Sloan asked, covering her hand with his.

"Better."

"No more guilt trips?"

Her eyes grew round at the gently stated question. "How did you know?"

The gentleness touched his eyes. "I know you. When

you were talking with your cousin about your grandmother, I could hear it in your voice, see it in your face.''

"Grandma could be very stubborn. Even when Anna suggested seeing Dr. Hatters in Flagstaff about a month ago, Grandma wouldn't. Almost all of her life she had lived with a doctor, and yet she hated to admit she was ever sick. Do you think she left Spencerville because she knew something was wrong?''

"There are some people who would like to die in peace and never see the inside of a hospital. She might have. But you can't forget that it was her choice.''

The waitress placed their breakfast before them. Sloan squeezed Kendall's hand reassuringly, then released it. She hadn't eaten much in the past two days and was starved.

"Mmm. When I have the time to eat it, breakfast is my favorite meal,'' she commented, tasting the omelet.

"Speaking of food, have you taken those cooking lessons yet? You know I expect a good home-cooked meal the next time I visit Spencerville.''

"When is that going to be?'' She had meant to say it in a light cheerful tone, but instead, an immediacy crept into the question.

"Thanksgiving would be the earliest, I'm afraid. Missi's birthday is in two weeks and I'm flying down to Atlanta for a few days to be with her. With all this traveling, I'll be behind in my work.''

"And I thought doctors worked hard.'' Kendall laughed but it was forced.

"Throughout this project I've had my share of problems, but I've never thought much about them until now, when I'm trying to get a few days off to fly down to see you. Just last week one of my hardest-working staff members left the project and I'm looking around frantically for a replacement. Guess who does his work until I find one.''

"You?''

"Right. Can you come to St. Louis before Thanksgiving?''

"I'll try to arrange some time, possibly in three weeks.''

"And I'll try not to have a boring faculty barbecue to go to, Doc.''

They finished their breakfast, planning the rest of the day's activities, starting with a nap they both needed. As they left the dining room, Sloan drew Kendall to him with an arm about her shoulder.

"We should sit in front of the fireplace before we leave,'' Kendall said, glancing at the stone fireplace that beckoned lovers to nestle in front of it.

"Later. Much later,'' Sloan whispered as they climbed the stairs to their second-floor room.

After closing the door, Sloan turned to her, his arms resting on her shoulders. "Do you need any help undressing? I do a marvelous job of unbuttoning and unzipping.''

Kendall arched a brow mockingly. "You do?''

"I accredited my success to practice.''

"Oh, and who have you been practicing on?''

"You.''

His hand moved to the top button of her shirt and

worked it loose. Then it traveled lower until finally the material fell open to reveal her bra. Fleetingly, his fingers grazed the lace, then the bare skin, the touch electric to her senses. He slid his hands inside her shirt, pushing the fabric off her shoulders and down her arms until it lay in a pool at her feet.

Drawing her to him, he settled his mouth on hers while he unsnapped her bra in the back, freeing her breasts against the smoothness of his shirt.

"Now, let me show you what a quick learner I am," Kendall teased, stepping slightly away to unbutton his shirt.

In the same maddeningly slow pace as him, Kendall freed each button, then ran her hands over his chest in torturous movements that elicited a deep moan. Bending forward, she kissed his nipples while drawing the shirt off his shoulders and down his arms.

"Doc, don't you know that no teacher likes to be surpassed the first day of class?" he growled as he scooped her up into his arms and headed for the bed.

"I thought you were tired."

"I may be exhausted, but I'm not over the hill yet. There's still a lot of life left in this tired body. I'll sleep on the plane." He dropped her gently onto the bed. "Now, for lesson number two."

"Do you think I can handle all this in one day?" Her silver-gray eyes shone with mischief.

"I'll take it slow and easy and explain my every move. First, I'm going to unzip your jeans and remove them, as well as your panties." His voice was full of husky titillation.

He knelt on the bed next to her and lowered the zipper, then worked the denim material down her legs, stopping once to study her inner thighs with light, tantalizing caresses. After tossing the jeans toward their pile of clothes, he massaged her calves in sensual circles before moving to her knees. He found a hypersensitive spot and stroked, all the while his gaze fixed upon her face, carefully gauging her every reaction.

Finally Sloan's hands roamed over her thighs, pausing at her panties to touch her through the thin fabric, slipping a finger under the material, teasing her for a few agonizing seconds before withdrawing.

Then before she realized it, he had stripped her panties off her with one quick movement. "Next, I'm going to take in every inch of you with my eyes, hands and mouth. Before I'm through I could sculpture you blindfolded." His voice became gravelly, pitched very low.

His intense eyes, glowing with adoration, captured hers, absorbing their silvery light, before he began his leisurely examination of her features that were shrouded in a languid look of desire. His tender sweep down the length of her disrupted the pace of her breathing and sent her heartbeat dancing to a rapid tempo.

When his pleasure-hazed eyes returned to seize her rapt attention again, she put her hands on the sides of his face and tried to drag him to her to end his blissful torment. But he held himself a breath away from her mouth, his scent engulfing her in a swirling mist of radiant sensations.

"Class isn't over yet," he whispered, moving his lips

in a light murmur down toward her neck before pulling away.

"Don't stop," Kendall moaned. She yearned for the feel of his lips on her, yet he was sitting up again.

"Now, I want to feel every inch of you," he said as he started at her toes and began to massage her with a mind-shattering sorcery. His hands kneaded, stroked, caressed her, a poignant, dizzying contact that made her hold on to reality—evasive, fragile.

By the time he had reached her breasts, she felt drenched with the exquisite rapture of his sensual exploration. When he took first one nipple, then the other, between his teeth and gently nibbled, she arched toward him, closing her eyes briefly to savor the quivering sensation that sped to every part of her.

"I want to taste every inch of you," came his whispered voice, as though he were at the other end of a long tunnel.

He showered her with kisses that were jeweled with words of love. "I will make you cry out with your need for me. I will possess you totally. I will love you fully."

Through a passion-drugged daze, Kendall moaned, "You're from Missouri. Show me. Now!"

Quickly, without words, he covered her with his body. His slow entrance was wildly sweet as he filled her. The sheer sensuality drove them toward a frenzied union, Kendall's fingers fervently grasping Sloan's shoulders.

It was several minutes before either one had his breathing under control and was able to speak. Still a silence prevailed as Sloan tenderly cradled Kendall to him and she fell into a deep sleep.

The shadows of a late afternoon slanted across the room when Kendall awakened within Sloan's loose embrace, a blanket thrown over their naked bodies. For a long moment she watched Sloan's features cloaked in sleep. Several times she had to resist the urge to awaken him. She knew how much he needed his sleep, yet their time together was growing short.

She moved away, intending to take a bath while he slept. Sloan's hand on her arm stopped her and hauled her back against the granite strength of his body.

"I'm still not warm, Doc. I think it will take hours to warm my blood enough before you can leave this bed."

"Sorry." Kendall wiggled free of Sloan's hold. "I want to see that sunset I missed yesterday."

She scurried into the bathroom and turned on the faucets in the bathtub. Kendall had just lowered herself into the water, scented with a bath oil, when Sloan appeared in the doorway with an appealing look of sleepiness still in his dark eyes, as if he were reliving his seductive dreams of moments before. Advancing into the room, his gaze locked with hers, he joined her in the tub.

Their laughter permeated the air as each looked at the precarious level of water that threatened at any moment to spill over onto the floor.

"Do you have a fetish about cramped bathing facilities?" Kendall finally asked, reaching around Sloan to let some of the water out of the tub. Their arms brushed; the tingling response could not be ignored.

"Only with you, Doc. Don't you think this is cozy?"

"Cozy wasn't the word I had in mind."

Under the water his hand discovered her thigh and began stroking it. The temperature of the water seemed to soar, and Kendall's body instantly flamed with heated sensations.

"Don't you think it's time the teacher tested his pupil's knowledge?" Sloan asked, sliding toward Kendall until he was stretched out on top of her, his hands and mouth beginning an agonizingly delightful journey over her body. "My God, Kendall, I don't know how I'm going to make it for three weeks without you."

Chapter Twelve

I'm sorry, Sloan, but Flora had a stroke a few hours ago. I'm at the hospital in Little Rock with her now. I won't be able to come this weekend."

"Can't someone else take over for the weekend, Kendall?" Sloan hated himself for asking the question, but he hadn't been able to sleep much since returning from Arizona. He missed Kendall, and after four months it was beginning to exact a heavy toll on him emotionally.

"Flora is frightened and has never known another doctor except a Spencer. I can't leave her, Sloan. Don't ask me to."

"I know that wasn't fair, but I was counting on seeing you tomorrow."

"Will you still be able to come for Thanksgiving?"

"Yes. No matter what happens I'll be there, Doc. That's a promise you can count on."

"I have to get back to Flora. I love you, Sloan." A tightness in her throat made each word an effort to speak.

"And I love you, darling."

For a long time after hanging up the phone, Sloan sat in the only room in his house that he could call his own—the den. He stared at the blaze in the fireplace that threw shadows on the wall and thought of that evening at the El Tovar, when they had nestled before the huge fireplace in the lobby and had talked for hours, late into the night while everyone else had slept. Then they had strolled back to their room and again had made love with a passion that had eclipsed their previous union. He needed that now.

At first he had thought the times they had spent together would be enough to carry him through, but he was discovering it wasn't enough. He wasn't sure if he could ever get enough of Kendall.

After seeing Missi the past weekend, he knew he wanted to be a part of a family, to have a wife and children. Glancing around the den, the empty quiet assailing him, he felt trapped in his loneliness. During Thanksgiving weekend Kendall and he had to come to some kind of satisfying agreement. He couldn't leave his job, but surely she could practice in St. Louis. It might not be quite the same, but she had to!

"I told you I was bound and determined to spend Thanksgiving with the love of my life." Sloan kissed her lightly on the mouth before stepping into the living room, exhaustion etched deeply into his features.

"I was so worried, Sloan. I don't like the idea of your flying down here this late at night. You should have waited until tomorrow morning."

"And miss a few hours with you? No way, lady. Besides, I've been flying for years and feel perfectly safe in my plane at night."

Kendall frowned. "You're not the one on the ground worrying. You look horrible, Sloan."

"Thanks. A guy always loves to hear that when he hasn't seen his woman in weeks." A wry grin sparked his dull eyes briefly.

With her hands on her hips, Kendall faced him. "Well, as your doctor I prescribe rest, hours of it."

He shortened the distance between them, nipping at her neck teasingly. "Well, Doc, I have to heartily agree with you—that is, if you'll hold my hand. I hope you got an A in bedside manners."

Suddenly Kendall threw her arms around Sloan, hugging him fiercely, as if she were reassuring herself that he was actually standing in her living room and wasn't a figment of her imagination. "I'll hold your hand all night if you want."

"Oh, darling, I've missed you so much," he whispered against her hair, lifting her slightly off the floor as he brought her even closer to him, his mouth seeking hers.

The kiss began gently but quickly evolved into a savage assault to feel, taste, possess the other. Her body was molded to his, his wiry hardness the strength that held them upright in the storm of their passion.

They finally parted long enough to make their way into Kendall's bedroom, where they both hurriedly undressed, almost frantically, as though they were dreaming and at any moment they would wake up and find themselves alone. Weeks of yearning culminated in a wild joining that was excitely intense.

"I'd give you an A-plus anytime, Doc," Sloan murmured, pulling her to him afterward, his eyes drifting closed as exhaustion claimed him.

The faint scent of turkey and coffee tantalized his senses as Sloan rolled over, automatically reaching out to touch Kendall as he had done in the past weeks. Like so many times in the past, though, his hand came in contact with the coldness of the sheet. His eyes snapped open to stare at the empty place next to him. For a confusing moment he wondered if he had dreamed seeing Kendall the night before and of the love they had made. Then he scanned her bedroom, bright with sunlight, and he knew he hadn't.

Tossing back the sheet and swinging his legs off the bed, Sloan stood and stepped into his jeans. He found Kendall at the kitchen sink, washing some broccoli.

The skin on the back of her neck prickled. Even before she twisted about, Kendall knew Sloan was standing in the doorway watching her. The dark force of his gaze riveted to the gray of hers.

"Good morning, Doc." His blond hair was tousled; his eyes still held a lazy look of sleep.

"It's good afternoon. I was about to come in and see if you were still breathing. Our Thanksgiving dinner is almost ready. And for dessert I baked you a chocolate cake to satisfy your insatiable sweet tooth."

"You really did learn to cook!"

"Don't act so surprised. I had to or starve. After a month of TV dinners I had had my fill of frozen meals and decided I'd better start learning to cook. Besides, I lost that bet to you, and I always pay my debts, sir. Did you doubt me?"

The smile that had been flirting at the corners of his mouth vanished. "You never told me you were learning." There was an added tenseness to his body as he pushed himself away from the doorframe and advanced into the kitchen.

"I wanted to surprise you with my hidden talents. I think my grandmother rubbed off on me, after all." The lightness in her voice was forced; her smile was glued on her face as if it would crack at any moment. Slowly, though, a distressed look altered her expression when Sloan didn't return the smile.

"Dammit, Kendall, I've missed so much of the everyday things in your life. What else new have you done that I don't know about?"

Cried myself to sleep many nights when I wanted to be held by you, made love to, Kendall thought. This weekend they had to come to a decision about their future, a compromise. She knew in the beginning a long-distance relationship wasn't for her. Maybe he could find a job in Little Rock. Surely someone else could carry on his work with his project.

"Nothing," she finally answered, turning back around to finish washing the broccoli. With a great effort she masked her anguish behind a neutral expression.

"Can I help?" His voice was rough.

"No. If you want to take a shower, you have time," Kendall said in a monotone, all the while placing the broccoli into a pot to steam.

"Okay. But, Kendall, we need to talk later."

Kendall's back grew rigid; her hands stopped in midair. "I agree."

She didn't relax even when she heard Sloan leave the kitchen. She felt wooden, straight and tall like a pine tree waiting to be axed down.

Sloan returned to the kitchen as Kendall finished setting the table, the dinner warm and ready on the stove. Glancing up, she inhaled a deep breath at the sight of him. Dressed in a black turtleneck sweater and tan pants, he looked virile, his male presence devastatingly attractive. His hair was still damp from the shower, and Kendall touched a lock on his forehead, smoothing it back into place.

"Your timing is perfect, Sloan Hunter. I've just finished everything."

"And I hurried as fast as I could, so I could help you." Mock disappointment gleamed in his dark eyes. "Now, all I have to figure out is what I'm going to do to get out of washing the dishes afterward."

"Oh, I'm sure you'll come up with something."

"What I'm thinking of doing involves two people." Desire darkened his eyes as he pushed back her chair and indicated she should be seated. "You've been working all morning. I'll serve you."

Kendall watched Sloan dish the food into bowls to place on the table. His movements were smooth, controlled, while her hands were trembling. While Sloan had been taking a shower, she had gone over and over their problem, yet no satisfying answer had come to mind.

"When will Flora come home?" Sloan asked as he sat down and passed her the platter with the turkey on it, then poured white wine into their glasses.

"Next week, if everything goes all right. I hope now she'll take her blood-pressure pills. She still has trouble talking, but most of her mobility is back. How's Missi doing? You know she has started writing me. She really misses Grandma."

What were they doing? Kendall wondered with dismay. All these questions had already been asked and answered over the phone. Of course, they were stalling the inevitable, avoiding the real issue.

They looked into each other's eyes at the same time, their actions halting as though they had instantly been frozen.

"Kendall . . ." Sloan paused, a frown descending over his features.

"Yes?" Kendall placed the bowl she had been holding on the table, the trembling in her hands spreading over her.

He shook his head. "Nothing." There was another lengthy pause before he continued: "Missi is fine. I talked with her yesterday before coming down here.

Sandra is getting better, but, of course, not fast enough for Missi. I think things are working out, though. Missi has a great art teacher at school who has taken an interest in her. That's helped.''

"Good," Kendall murmured, then began to eat, feeling suddenly as if they were polite strangers.

She had touched very little of her dinner when Sloan put his fork down on his plate, the sound startling her in the quiet of the kitchen. She looked up.

"I don't think it can wait," Sloan stated, bolting down his glass of wine in several swallows. His attention became engrossed in the bottom of the glass, the strong slope of his mouth twisting downward in a grim expression.

"No! Not now, Sloan!" Kendall suddenly said with a force that she hadn't thought herself capable of.

He combed his fingers through his hair, blond waves feathering back from his face in negligent order. "Do you want to go on this way?"

Kendall stood, pushing back her chair. Staring down at him, she noticed that his face registered no emotion now as he waited for her answer. His sudden overall impression of cool serenity, while her emotions were in tatters, unnerved her and she had to escape. Fleeing the kitchen, she didn't stop until she was outside on the porch, collapsing into the swing.

The cold air whipped at her, chilling her in spite of the sunlight. She felt like a time bomb, methodically ticking away, merely waiting for the explosion.

"Kendall?"

The incredibly tender smile in his eyes pained her

more than the tone of desperation. "Sloan, I want to be happy this weekend. Please, don't say anything now."

He didn't answer her, but instead sat next to her, his presence a calm permanence that she found she needed very much. The fine-tuned tension in his body slowly ebbed as he held her to him in silence.

"It can wait, Kendall. But we will have to face it soon."

"I know," she whispered against his shoulder, the comfort of his arms warming her.

Then without a word, Sloan stood and pulled Kendall to her feet, guiding her toward the front door. Inside the house, he turned toward her. "I hope you have nothing planned for this weekend, because I have no intention of leaving this place. In fact, we may not leave the bedroom." The look of mischievous delight deepened the laugh lines at the corners of his eyes.

"What about eating?"

"You mean you would rather eat than make love with me!"

"The dinner! All my work! It's getting cold." Kendall started for the kitchen, but Sloan's hand on her wrist prevented her from moving a foot.

"I know you went to a lot of trouble preparing the Thanksgiving dinner, and I promise I'll give you an opportunity to display your hidden talents another time. But, lady, that isn't what is foremost on my mind at the moment."

Kendall laughed, a pure delicious sound that completely erased the tension of moments before. "It isn't?"

Sloan caught her to him, muttering in a low growl, "No, but I'd be glad to show you what is."

His fingers went to the top button of her shirt, loosening it, then moving down to the next one. He pushed the material aside to cup her bare breasts, then bent to roll a tautened nipple between his lips, his tongue flicking over it. When he turned his attention to the other nipple, a spark of heat in her loins produced an exquisite pleasure. Slipping her shirt off her, Sloan crushed her to him, his mouth closing over hers.

The harsh ring of the phone lanced into the stillness, parting them instantly.

"Don't answer it," Sloan muttered in a passion-coated voice as he sought to capture Kendall against him again.

"I have to, Sloan. I'm a doctor."

Reluctantly he let her go, and she walked into the den to pick up the phone. She was aware of the fact that Sloan had followed her as she said, "Dr. Spencer speaking."

"We need you right away," the sheriff said in an urgent tone. "There's been a bus accident a mile outside of town on the state highway to Little Rock. It's bad, Kendall. The bus swerved to miss a cow and turned over in a ditch."

"I'll be right there." Kendall hung up and spun around to face Sloan, walking swiftly toward the living room, where her shirt was. "That was Kirk. There's been a bus accident and I don't know how long I'll be."

"Do you want me to go with you?"

"No. I'll try to get back as fast as I can." Kendall was buttoning her shirt as she walked to the closet to get her jacket.

"Maybe I can help."

"There's probably already too many people there, but you can call Bonnie for me. I don't know if Kirk did, and I'll need her. Her number is by the phone in the den. Tell her to be at the clinic right away." Kendall picked up her medical bag and was out the door before Sloan could answer.

Sloan stood in the center of the living room motionless for several minutes. Only moments before he had been holding Kendall, kissing her, undressing her. Now she was gone. When she had slammed her front door shut, it was as if visiting day was over and he had been locked up again in his prison cell. She hadn't even wanted his help. Not only did they live miles apart, but when they were together, her job often demanded her time. It was hard enough adjusting to their lengthy separations, but this added problem was becoming too much for him to handle.

Slowly he made his way into the den and called Bonnie, giving her the necessary information. Again, he was struck with the fact he was on the outside looking in. After his call to Bonnie, he decided to clean up the kitchen, then wait for Kendall's return.

An hour later he sat in a chair in the den, watching a football game on the television set in front of him. If someone had asked him who won the game, Sloan wouldn't have been able to tell him.

Finally, tired of sitting, he flipped off the TV and headed for the kitchen to fix himself a turkey sandwich. Glancing at the clock on the wall, he noticed it was nine o'clock.

At eleven he lay down on the bed in Kendall's bedroom to rest until she came home. He closed his eyes for a moment and didn't open them until the grayish tint of dawn spread through the sky and into the room.

His arm was flung over his forehead, shadowing his eyes. He knew before he looked that Kendall wasn't in the house. He touched the vacant place next to him, a yearning to hold Kendall growing into a full-fledged hunger.

Sloan felt as though his body were glued to the bed. He didn't want to get up and start the day without Kendall. In the back of his mind he couldn't rid himself of the feeling that it would be a long, lonely day.

Finally, when shafts of sunlight poured through the windowpane, Sloan shaved, showered and dressed, then began the waiting all over again.

Sloan had worn a path in the carpet by the time darkness had descended and he had to switch on a light in the living room. He had tried calling the clinic earlier, but Kendall had driven into Little Rock late the day before with the last of the patients who had been transported to the hospital there.

The slam of a car door brought a halt to his pacing. He turned as Kendall stepped into the house. Exhaustion lined her features and she wearily made her way into the living room, dropping her bag in a chair by the door.

Sloan waited for her to speak.

His gaze snared Kendall's, and she paused while shrugging out of her jacket, her arms falling to her sides again. Her emotions were scattered in a thousand different directions, and she couldn't seem to grasp onto a single train of thought. A silence pulsated between them as they stared at each other.

"How bad was it?" Sloan asked, releasing her gaze as his took in the paleness in her cheeks, the slight sag to her shoulders.

"Five people were critically injured, three seriously and ten others have been hospitalized in fair condition or for observation. A few I was able to treat and release." Her restraint that had kept her going for thirty hours snapped, and she collapsed against Sloan.

Steel fingers held her upright against him for a few seconds before Sloan removed her jacket, then lifted her up into his arms and carried her into the bedroom. "Did you get any rest?"

"No. It was a nightmare. But if I hadn't arrived so quickly I think a few of them wouldn't have made it. It's still touch and go for a couple, but at least now they have a chance."

Sloan gently laid Kendall on her bed, then sat next to her, unbuttoning and slipping off her shirt, which had dried blood on it. Rolling her over onto her stomach, he began to massage her tensed muscles, kneading the soreness from her shoulders first.

"There was a family from Spencerville on the bus. We nearly lost Kathy, the mother. I grew up and went to

school with her. If anything had happened to her . . .''
The magic of Sloan's fingers stole the rest of her
sentence as a haze of sleep swirled about her and
whisked her away into a dreamless world.

A prickly awareness tingled through Kendall, drawing
her away from the world of her dreams and toward
wakefulness. She nestled deeper into the covers, resist-
ing the strong pull to wake up. Slowly, her eyes drifted
open.

At first she thought she was alone in the darkened
bedroom, but as her eyes adjusted to the blackness, she
saw, sitting in the chair by her bed, a figure whose hands
were laced together in a steeple, his chin resting on
them.

''Sloan?''

He disengaged himself from his relaxed poise and
switched on the bedside lamp. A bright light flooded the
room, causing Kendall to blink and look down away
from the lamp. That was when she noticed Sloan's
suitcase sitting by the chair. Her startled gaze flew to his
face.

''Is something wrong? Why are you leaving?'' Her
voice was low, barely working.

Sloan leaned forward, placing his elbows on his
knees, his arms dangling down between his legs. ''The
hospital called thirty minutes ago. Kathy went into
emergency surgery. Dr. Mathews is operating. But
there's no need for you to be at the hospital for a few
hours, so I didn't wake you right away. I packed first.''

Kendall struggled to a sitting position, her back

against the bed board. She was torn between her duty and her need to talk with Sloan.

"You'd better call the hospital first, Kendall. Then we'll talk." His face was an unyielding mask, his voice deadly quiet, frosting her with its icy calm.

As she reached for the phone, her hands quaked and she nearly dropped the receiver. She didn't meet Sloan's eyes as she placed her call through to the hospital. After checking on Kathy's status, Kendall hung up and finally looked toward Sloan.

"I need to be at the hospital. I want to be there when she comes out of surgery. The nurse estimates it will be at least another two hours, though." She couldn't keep her voice from quavering.

"I'm leaving, Kendall."

"Why? I hope I have to be gone only a few hours."

"You don't know that for sure."

"Kathy is my patient!" Kendall sat straight up in bed, her hands clenched at her sides.

"I'm aware of that," Sloan said, his voice too calm.

"Are you asking me to make a choice between my patients and you?"

"How do you want me to play this scene, Kendall? Be noble or tell you what's in my heart." Sloan rose, towering over her.

A great pressure in her chest tightened its hold and she took several deep breaths, but nothing relieved the feeling of suffocation. She felt as though she were underwater and had no air left in her scuba tank.

"The truth," she murmured, glancing away. She

couldn't look at the hard determination in his features. Instead, she stared out the window at the darkness of an early hour.

"I honestly thought I could handle this situation with us living in two different places, but I'm finding I can't. I kept telling you I believed things would work out for us, because I was trying to convince myself they would. I think in the back of my mind I was praying you would move to St. Louis, but I can see you won't." Sloan moved toward the end of the bed, gripping the post, his knuckles white. "A few stolen days every couple of months isn't enough for me. I have to have more, Kendall. I want a family and a home."

"Oh, I see. You thought since I was the woman that I should be the one to give up my job and come live with you in St. Louis. I shouldn't be surprised that it came down to this. I told you at the beginning it would."

His expression was tempered with steel. "Can you deny that you hoped I would leave my position and move down here?"

"No, but . . ."

"There are no buts. We both wanted the other to give up his job when in our hearts we knew we wouldn't, we couldn't right now. We both made a commitment we can't discard easily. I have to feel important to the woman I love, that I come first, and frankly at the moment I don't with you. I've already gone through one relationship that left its scars. I don't want to face another one and it would be better to end everything now rather than months from now."

The hardness in his features softened slightly as their gazes embraced across the expanse of the bed. Kendall was speechless, the combination of shock and pain stealing her voice.

"We can both get on with our lives and maybe find some kind of happiness. This isn't enough for you or me." He gestured widely with his arms.

Kendall swallowed with difficulty. "Do you think you'll find happiness?"

"Yes—no. Dammit, Kendall, I don't know. But at least I won't be going in two different directions all the time. This town is your life, your home. You won't, and I know in my heart that I can't ask you to leave Spencerville. Good-bye, Doc."

Swiftly he walked to the bedside. Grasping her upper arms, Sloan lifted her slightly off the bed, angling his head to fit his mouth tenderly to hers. She felt his heart pound against her as though its beats were passing from his body into hers. Then as quickly as he had kissed her, he relinquished his possession, but his gaze stayed on her. Lightly he touched her cheek with a trembling finger, tracing the outline of her mouth, his eyelids sliding closed for a heart-rending moment. Then abruptly he turned, picked up his suitcase and left. The sound of the door shutting quietly behind him reverberated like the after-shocks of an earthquake.

Kendall dug her teeth into her lower lip, trying to expunge the feel of his mouth on hers. She had known this was coming, perhaps from the very beginning, but she wasn't emotionally prepared for it. She wasn't sure she ever would be. When he had walked out that door, he had taken a part of her with him, a part necessary for her happiness, her love.

"Damn him to hell! Why did he make me love him?"

Tears fell onto her cheeks and she furiously scrubbed at them. He had left her and if it took all her willpower, she wouldn't cry over him. But as she hugged her pillow to her, she tasted the salt of her tears.

Chapter Thirteen

There were times lately that Kendall doubted she could think rationally anymore. She was sitting in a conference room in a St. Louis hotel at a medical convention with Dr. Sloan Hunter as one of the guest speakers. Her first reaction had been not to attend the medical convention, but as her anger toward Sloan had faded, she couldn't resist coming and possibly seeing him again. What she hoped to gain from it she didn't know.

It had been six weeks since he had left and she hadn't heard from him. On Christmas Day she had been so depressed that she hadn't visited her neighbors as she usually did every year. The phone had rung many times that day, but she hadn't answered because in her heart she had known none of the callers had been Sloan, and that had been the only person she had wanted to talk to.

After Sloan's speech, which was next on the agenda,

she was supposed to meet with Dr. Roberts, who had wanted to speak to her at the convention. Dr. Roberts had stopped her in the lobby the day before and had arranged the meeting that had sparked her interest. However, he hadn't had the time to go into the reason for the meeting then because he had been late for a lunch date with his son.

Kendall finished her cup of coffee and placed it on the table before making her way toward her seat again. The meeting was about to begin and her heartbeat increased its pace. She searched the room for Sloan and found him entering by a side door. Her heart skipped a beat, then began to hammer even faster. Their gazes collided but didn't hold as Sloan looked away, as if he didn't know her and she was just one of many in the audience.

At that moment she knew she had made a mistake in coming to the medical convention. She wanted to slip away from the meeting, but she saw no way to do it unnoticed. And her pride wouldn't allow her to climb over five people's legs and walk down the aisle to the door.

Kendall rubbed her clammy palms together as the chairman introduced Sloan. She felt cold. Sloan's eyes swept the audience and coolly rested on her for a brief second before moving away.

"I'm honored to have been asked to speak today about my current research on lung cancer."

The sound of his voice brought back a profusion of emotions. She relived in her mind the agony and loneliness of that first week after he had left when she had sat by the phone wanting to pick it up and call him, but instead, waiting for him to call her. The silence of her house had eaten into her until she hardly ever stayed there anymore. Often she would sleep at the clinic because each time she looked at her bed, she would remember the ecstasy she had felt in Sloan's arms, then the emptiness of that first night after he had left her.

In fact, everywhere she went in Spencerville, memories assaulted her. Each place they had been twisted the knife of painful longing deeper into her heart. She used to love Spencerville, but lately her hometown had become a prison, something she had to escape if she were ever to proceed with her life and have any happiness at all.

She was diligently looking for someone whom the people in Spencerville would accept to take over her practice. That was one of the reasons she had decided to come to the medical convention—that and the fact that she was going to meet with Dr. Hatters of Flagstaff.

Dr. Hatters was the doctor for the Indian village where her cousin lived and her grandmother had died. He held a clinic at the village two times a week, besides his practice in Flagstaff. Anna and she had been writing ever since her grandmother's death. Anna had mentioned in her last letter that Dr. Hatters would be attending the convention. Lately an idea had begun to form in her mind, but it hinged on two things, finding another doctor for Spencerville and being accepted by Dr. Hatters, who was approaching sixty and had no partners in his practice. She wanted desperately to start over fresh and bury herself in her work.

The sound of the applause focused Kendall's thoughts

on the present; Sloan stood at the podium not three rows from her. She ached to touch him, to feel the pressure of his lips on hers again. Standing abruptly, she sought to escape now that the meeting was starting to break up.

"Dr. Spencer."

Kendall stopped and slowly turned toward the man behind her.

"This afternoon I'll be a few minutes late. Can we make it two o'clock instead of one-thirty?" Dr. Roberts asked.

They had moved out of the way of the crowd toward the front of the room as Dr. Roberts continued: "My son has to return to work and I'm driving him to the airport right now."

"That will be fine, Dr. Roberts. I'll be in the coffee shop at two, and if you're delayed at the airport, don't worry."

"Thank you, Dr. Spencer."

Kendall turned away and started for the nearest door when she ran into Sloan, who was also trying to leave by the side door. Her gaze traveled from his chest— sheathed in a brown wool suit coat and beige silk shirt—to his chin, then to his mouth, set in a grim line, not a hint of a smile anywhere.

"Sloan." Her throat closed around his name.

"Kendall," he acknowledged crisply. Then he hesitated before adding, "Thank you for sending Missi one of your grandmother's pieces of pottery for Christmas. She adored the present."

Someone behind Kendall knocked into her, pushing her toward Sloan, whose hand shot out to steady her. For

a brief moment as his hand held her arm, each looking
deeply into the other's eyes, it was as if no one else was
in the room. Without thinking, she raised her hand to
touch his jaw. He flinched, the crush on her arm easing
abruptly as he yanked his hand away.

His mouth dipped into a harsh frown. A spearing
tension stirred the air about them, as if it might snap
suddenly, piercing her with its wounding shards. She felt
like one of his glass figurines that he had picked up and
thrown against the wall, smashing it into a thousand
pieces.

Then his fingers, like steel talons, clasped her arm
again and he pulled her farther away from the crowd into
the corner by the side door. "Why in the hell did you
come to St. Louis?" His dark eyes were like dry ice,
burning and cold at the same time.

Her back stiffened with pride. "I'll be damned if
you'll keep me away from a medical convention I usually
attend every year." The frost in her voice matched the
glacial temperature in his eyes.

Suddenly a proud, aloof mantle shielded his thoughts,
his hand dropping to his side as though he had been
contaminated by her touch. "Good day, Dr. Spencer."

He turned on his heel and strode away, and Kendall
felt the loss deep in her soul. Inside, her emotions
crumbled into dust. She had grown so dependent on
Sloan that his withdrawal had hurt her more than she had
ever imagined anything could. Chills racked her body,
and she hurriedly left the conference to seek the privacy
of her hotel room.

In the elevator she bolstered herself with a deep

breath, pushing a few stray strands of hair away from her face with a trembling hand. She had never thought she could hate as she hated Sloan at that moment. She hated him for making her love him, for not fighting hard enough for their love, and for destroying that love in the end.

When she entered her hotel room, she sat on the bed, her muscles locked. She realized she had still hoped they would get back together. She had dared to even dream of their meeting here in St. Louis, where everything would be forgotten but their love for each other.

"Love!" She spat out the word in disgust.

But deep within her she wanted to see Sloan again, touch him, hold him.

Kendall stayed in her room until two o'clock doing anything to keep herself busy, even packing, although she wasn't leaving until the next day at noon. When she stepped off the elevator, she scanned the lobby before crossing to the coffee shop. She couldn't withstand another meeting with Sloan. That much she had discovered earlier.

Phil Roberts was already seated in a booth by the window and waved to her as she entered the coffee shop. As she walked toward the booth, she caught a glimpse of Sloan excusing himself from a table of men on the opposite side of the room. The blaze in his eyes could only be interpreted as anger, his mouth a slash of barely controlled fury.

Kendall yanked her gaze away from his roughly hewn profile, which was chiseled in stone, and quickly covered the rest of the distance to the booth.

Seated across from Dr. Roberts, with her order for coffee given to the waitress, Kendall finally asked, "What did you want to see me about?"

"I've heard you're still looking for a partner for your practice in Spencerville. I'd like to move back there."

Those words would have brought her ecstatic joy two months before; now all they did was bring her relief that she could leave Spencerville and start all over somewhere else, where memories of Sloan wouldn't exist.

"Actually, I want someone to take over my practice in Spencerville. There's room for two doctors because the population is growing, but one can handle it for a while."

"That's great. My son loves the area and will be through with his internship within the year." His eyes sparkled with excitement.

"If we can work things out, I would stay on for a few months as an adjustment period."

The waitress brought them their coffee and they began to discuss Spencerville and Kendall's practice. By the time she left Dr. Roberts in the lobby, they had set up a date for him to come to Spencerville to check things out. She walked toward the elevator, her steps light for the first time in weeks. She liked Phil Roberts and felt the townspeople would also. This trip might have been the end for her and Sloan, but it also gave her the chance for a new beginning, and she was determined to take it.

In the middle of her office, Kendall turned slowly around, looking at all of her possessions boxed up and ready to be moved to her house. The first day of April she would be leaving Spencerville. In two weeks she was due to start work with Dr. Hatters in Flagstaff. She had family there and a chance to throw herself into her work.

"Kendall, are you through with everything in here?" Bonnie asked from the doorway. "Kirk will be here in a few minutes to take these to your house."

Kendall scanned the bareness once more, the fact that she would be leaving Spencerville in a few days finally sinking in. For the past month she had been going through the motions of packing, saying good-byes, but only a part of her had. The other part had stood away, watching as she had one by one severed her ties with her past.

"Yes, I'm through. I only have Flora to see. Then everything will be Phil's."

"Are you positive, Kendall? I know we've gone through this, but why are you leaving?"

"Spencerville is in great hands. The people love Dr. Roberts. I couldn't have found a better doctor to take over." Kendall leaned back against her desk, her expression strained with a guarded look.

"Then at least go to St. Louis. Why Flagstaff?" Bonnie walked into the office and shut the door.

"Don't, Bonnie. It's hard enough leaving without all these questions."

"Call Sloan."

"No! Never!" Kendall tensed, her hold on her desk tightening painfully.

"You know you can now. You could practice in St. Louis."

"That's not possible," Kendall answered in a choked whisper. "I saw him in St. Louis in January, and believe me, there are no feelings left. He killed them. He couldn't understand there would be times my patients would have to come first, no matter what. I would never be happy in St. Louis. I like small towns, open spaces, and Arizona has those for me."

"Are you looking for excuses not to call him? I know you, Kendall, and you don't commit lightly."

The door opened and Kirk entered the office. Relieved, Kendall quickly began directing Kirk in what to do as she picked up a box herself.

"I know I stick my nose into other people's business when I shouldn't. I won't say another thing." Bonnie began carrying out a box, adding as they stepped outside, "Don't forget the farewell party Friday night."

"I won't. If I don't show up, I know you'll personally come over and drag me to the party."

Bonnie laughed. "Maybe not me, but Kirk will."

As they walked back into the building, Flora arrived for her appointment. Flora had insisted on seeing Kendall for this last appointment, even though most people were now seeing Dr. Roberts. Kendall had arranged for Phil to come into the examination room at the end to speak with Flora. She knew the older woman had some reservations about changing doctors. Flora was a lot like Maria had been about doctors. When Flora had had her stroke, it had worn Kendall out going back and forth to the hospital, because when Flora was conscious, she wouldn't let another doctor look at her.

After examining Flora, Kendall wrote out a prescription for the older woman's medicine, then turned to hand it to her. Flora took the piece of paper and stuffed it into her purse.

"I can't believe a Spencer won't be the doctor for this town. If Maria were here, she . . ."

"Flora, my grandmother would have approved of this move. Give Dr. Roberts a chance."

"He's a stranger." Flora's frown grew into a scowl.

"He was born in Spencerville."

"But he moved away when he was young. I don't know him." Stubbornness marked deeper lines into her aged face.

"Have you given the man a chance? Everyone else likes him."

"Maria left for Arizona. Why do you have to?"

"Because, like Grandma, part of my heritage is there, too."

"Humph!" Flora folded her arms across her chest and straightened, as though she were readying herself for battle.

"Please, Flora, give Dr. Roberts a chance. I've asked him to come in here to speak to you. Will you listen?"

"Humph!" She looked away out the window.

Kendall sighed, punching the intercom button and asking Bonnie to send in Dr. Roberts. A moment later he opened the door and stepped into the examination room.

Quickly he assessed the situation. "I've wanted to speak to you again for some time, Mrs. Baker. When I lived here as a child, I worshipped your husband as my only hero."

Flora blinked, pulling her gaze from the window and toward Dr. Roberts. "You did?"

"Yes. He was ten years older than I . . ."

Kendall left the room and walked toward her office. She knew in time Flora would accept Dr. Roberts. Inside her empty office, she retrieved her purse, feeling as though her professional business in Spencerville was completed. Friday night she would say her good-byes to the townspeople and then everything would be over.

The rest of Wednesday and all of Thursday Kendall spent packing up her belongings at the house. She had a hard time boxing up the things her grandmother had left behind when she had moved to Arizona. Kendall took extra care wrapping up each piece of Maria's pottery, tears clouding her vision as she remembered the times her grandmother had made each one.

On Friday morning Kendall only had her bedroom things left to pack. She dressed in old faded jeans and a T-shirt and started the last of her packing right after breakfast, determined to be finished that afternoon. She had the impulse to be on the road by Saturday instead of Sunday.

The sound of a sharp rap drew Kendall's attention toward the front door, her brow creasing in puzzlement. She wasn't expecting Kirk to help her until that afternoon.

When she opened the door, her startled eyes took in the hard planes of Sloan's face, carved with an iron hand, his bronzed skin stretched tautly over high cheekbones and a commanding jawline. For a few seconds her senses drank in the molded ruggedness of his features, leaner, more ruthless-looking than before.

The image of a shrewd predator dissolved as a warm smile transformed his face. "Aren't you going to invite me in?"

Kendall fought the automatic response to smile back at him, quickly erecting her defenses against the magnetism of his grin. "No. Why should I?"

"Because we need to talk, Kendall."

"You've already said all that I care to hear. Good day, Dr. Hunter."

Kendall went to slam the door in his face, but his arm and foot blocked her.

"I know I deserved that, but please hear me out."

"I think the meeting in St. Louis said all that needed to be said."

"I'm afraid it didn't even scratch the surface. Why didn't you tell me you were moving away from Spencerville?"

Sloan tried to inch his body through the partially opened door, but Kendall stood her ground. "I didn't know then. Besides, what difference could it have made? You made it quite obvious our relationship couldn't withstand distance or time. I believe Flagstaff is a bit farther away from St. Louis than Spencerville."

She frantically struggled to build the wall higher around her emotions, so no buried feelings could enter and destroy what fragile control she still had.

"May I come in, Kendall? I won't leave until we have had that talk."

"Then I'll call the sheriff." Her chin tilted at a defiant angle.

"Go ahead. Who do you think called me yesterday to tell me you were leaving Spencerville, that you had found a doctor months ago to practice here?"

"Bonnie. I could cheerfully wring her neck." With an exasperated shrug, Kendall stepped aside to allow Sloan into the house. "And I think I will tonight." Shutting the door, she faced Sloan, adding, "Hurry up and say what you came to say. Then I want you to leave me alone."

Leisurely he surveyed the room, with all the boxes piled up along the walls. "Have you got everything packed?"

"Quit the chitchat, Sloan. I have very little time to stand here waiting for you to get to the point, since I'm *not* through with my packing."

"The point is—I don't know where to begin. I have so much to say to you."

"How about condensing it into one short sentence, then leaving."

Sloan slowly ran his hand along the edge of a box, measuring her as though he were carefully calculating his next move. "That's not easy."

"Try, because I'm walking into my bedroom in ten seconds and I'm going to finish my packing without your assistance."

She stared at the war of emotions parading across Sloan's face while she silently counted to ten.

When she began to walk toward her bedroom, Sloan blurted out, "I need you so badly, Doc."

Kendall closed her eyes, glad her back was to Sloan. The sudden feeling of plunging helplessly into a bottomless abyss overwhelmed her and it took a minute for her to compose herself enough to say in a cool voice, "Okay, you've had your say. Now you're free to go."

"Damn you, Kendall! You can't dismiss what was between us so lightly. I know you still have feelings for me."

The male assurance in his voice irritated her and she grasped onto that fact to fuel her anger against him. Whirling around, she stabbed him with a contemptuous look, meant to cut him to ruthless shreds as her emotions had been over the last four months.

"Your nerve is colossal, Hunter. *I dismissed!* I think you have your facts backward. I'm not the one who walked out on our relationship." As she spoke, she advanced on him, a seething coldness in her eyes directed completely at him. Halting in front of him, only inches away, she poked him several times in the chest as she continued in a lethal-sounding voice, "You were. *You, Sloan!*"

His mouth slanted upward. "At least I can still arouse something in you."

"You're right there. My anger!"

"I think I arouse more than your anger, Doc."

His hand grazed her arm, his lean strength so close that Kendall suddenly realized the potent danger.

"I'm not 'Doc' to you. I am Dr. Spencer." She had intended to say those words with a stinging force, but instead they came out in a husky whisper. Her icy wall of anger couldn't withstand Sloan's overpowering presence. It had been so much easier to hate him while he was hundreds of miles away.

Slowly he lowered his head toward hers, his lips caressing hers lightly at first. Then swiftly he ground his mouth into hers with a demanding fire, propelling her backward a few steps until his arms enfolded her against him in a masterful embrace. Forcing his way past her clamped lips, he swept his tongue boldly into the sweet warmth of her mouth, gloriously persuasive. His kiss was branding, claiming, seductive, promising searing passion. But the most alluring element was being held again in his arms, close to his strong body, secure with the knowledge of her power to arouse him.

No longer able to resist his ardent persistence, Kendall clutched at Sloan, losing herself in the taste of him, in his masculine scent, in the muscular hardness of his body as he pressed her backward, guiding her toward the couch.

Somewhere in her numbed mind a protest formed and fought its need to be heard. Taking him by surprise, she jerked away from Sloan, placing the safety of a few feet between them.

"Please don't, Sloan."

"You can't deny you don't have feelings for me other than hate. You respond to me."

"Okay. I responded." Her breasts heaved as she dragged air into her lungs. "But it doesn't change our situation. These last four months I've had plenty of lonely nights to think about us, to think about what you said at Thanksgiving. You were right. Our situation was no good."

"Our situation may have been rotten, but we, as a couple, weren't. That was very right and good." He took a step toward her.

Kendall raised her hand to stop him. "Stay where you are, Sloan." She shook her head, as though to clear it of unwanted thoughts. "I can't think rationally when you're near me."

He grinned ruefully. "That was my intention—to sweep you off your feet and not to give you time to think."

"No, that wouldn't solve anything."

"Things have a way of working out."

"Oh, yes, you told me that once, then left me. I don't like your idea of 'working out.' "

"I have to chalk up that scene Thanksgiving weekend to a proud, very frustrated man."

"And the medical convention?"

"The same." His smile was full of self-irony. "God, Kendall, do you know what it did to me to see you in that conference room and know I couldn't have you? I'm not sure how I made it through that speech. I'm still amazed I put two coherent sentences together."

Kendall smiled.

"I like that."

"What?"

"Your smile. I've missed it. I've missed you, Kendall. I love you so much and no amount of distance or time is going to change that fact. That's what I've learned these last four, agonizing months. There comes a time when it hurts so much that you stop feeling. Christmas, even with Missi in St. Louis, was hell."

Kendall's determination not to love wavered when she saw his love for her in his dark eyes and he reached out to her to fill her with a warmth she hadn't felt in a long time.

"I've made arrangements to practice in Flagstaff, Sloan. I want to get to know my grandmother's people."

"Are you trying to replace one family with another?"

Kendall's gray eyes widened. "No," she slowly answered. "But I feel I owe it to my grandmother, who gave up her heritage and her people to give so much of herself to Spencerville."

"Will you spend your whole life serving others, never looking out for your own needs, desires?"

His questions were disquieting. Sitting down on the couch, Kendall leaned forward, her elbows resting on her thighs, her hands clasped together. "I'm a doctor, Sloan."

"Will that be your catch-all excuse for ignoring your feelings and needs?" Sloan sat next to her, his thigh touching the length of hers.

"I never really thought about it."

"I know. You never gave any thought to what you wanted. I could see and sense the war you waged within yourself over our relationship. I felt it so deeply because I fought my own battle with myself." He grasped her hands and twisted her about to face him. "Kendall, we can have both!"

"How?"

"I was on the phone all afternoon yesterday, and if I want that job at the institute in Phoenix, it's still open for me. They want me to start my own project, related to mine at the university.''

''But I'll be in Flagstaff or on the reservation, almost three hours away from Phoenix. That's still long distance in my book.'' She sagged back against the couch, doubt heavy in her voice.

''Have you forgotten that I own a plane and that I'm an excellent pilot? We can live in Flagstaff and you can commute to the reservation when you need to and I can fly to Phoenix. But the important part is that we will be living together in the same house as husband and wife.'' His voice was a gentle coercion, his eyes sensuous tethers. ''Will you marry me, Dr. Kendall Spencer?''

''What about your project at the university? Are you willing to leave it?''

''I want us to be married right away. I have a proposition to put to you.'' He brushed his lips across hers, then sat up straight, no longer touching her, his gaze trained on a spot on the far wall. ''I can't leave the project for at least six months, possibly nine. Will you come live in St. Louis for that time? Then we'll move to Arizona.''

''St. Louis?''

He half-turned to look at her, his eyes darkening. ''Kendall, I can't go through another four months without you. When Bonnie called yesterday, I saw a way for us to be together right now, today. I can't walk out on the project, at least not yet, and I can't live without you and be worth a damn.''

It took only a second for Kendall to reach a decision.

She threw her arms around Sloan's neck and kissed him fiercely on the mouth, whispering against his lips. "Yes. Yes, I'll marry you. Dr. Hatters has practiced this long without a partner. I'm sure he can wait a little longer."

"Are you sure, Kendall?"

"Are you sure?"

"The one thing I'm sure about is you. Yes, I'm very sure, Doc."

"Good. Now, I think I could use some assistance in the bedroom."

Sloan's hand went to the snap of her jeans. "What kind of assistance?"

"Packing, Sloan. Packing," Kendall said with a laugh.

"Are you sure that's the only thing?" He unsnapped her jeans and slid the zipper down, then slipped his hand inside.

Her pulse raced; her heartbeat accelerated. "Kirk will be here soon to help me load everything into my car and the U-Haul."

He toyed with the waistband of her panties before moving his hand under her T-shirt and up to cup her breast. "I told Bonnie we would be late tonight for the party and that I would help you pack."

"The party. I forgot about that. I'd better call Bonnie and tell her I'm not leaving for Arizona after all." Her words came out in a breathless whisper. Sloan had pulled up her shirt and was bending forward to flick his tongue over her breasts, her nipples hard with her mounting desire.

"That's okay. Bonnie's changed the party to an engagement celebration."

Kendall drew away slightly, forcing Sloan to look up at her. "You're very sure of yourself, Sloan Hunter."

"Not sure. Just very determined, Doc." His mouth muffled her next words as he stamped her his, pressing her back until she lay on the couch, his body covering hers.

Silhouette Special Edition. Romances for the woman who expects a little more out of love.

If you enjoyed this book, and you're ready for more great romance

...get 4 romance novels FREE when you become a Silhouette Special Edition home subscriber.

Act now and we'll send you four exciting Silhouette Special Edition romance novels. They're our gift to introduce you to our convenient home subscription service. Every month, we'll send you six new passion-filled Special Edition books. Look them over for 15 days. If you keep them, pay just $11.70 for all six. Or return them at no charge.

We'll mail your books to you two full months *before they are available anywhere else.* Plus, with every shipment, you'll receive the Silhouette Books Newsletter absolutely free. *And with Silhouette Special Edition there are never any shipping or handling charges.*

Mail the coupon today to get your four free books—and more romance than you ever bargained for.

Silhouette Special Edition is a service mark and a registered trademark of Simon & Schuster, Inc.

MAIL COUPON TODAY

Silhouette Special Edition℠
120 Brighton Road, P.O. Box 5020, Clifton, N.J. 07015

☐ Yes, please send me FREE and without obligation, 4 exciting Silhouette Special Edition romance novels. Unless you hear from me after I receive my 4 FREE BOOKS, please send me 6 new books to preview each month. I understand that you will bill me just $1.95 each for a total of $11.70—with no additional shipping, handling or other charges. **There is no minimum number of books that I must buy, and I can cancel anytime I wish.** The first 4 books are mine to keep, even if I never take a single additional book.

☐ Mrs. ☐ Miss ☐ Ms. ☐ Mr.   **BSS9R4**

Name	(please print)

Address	Apt. No.

City	State	Zip

Signature (If under 18, parent or guardian must sign.)

This offer, limited to one per customer, expires March 31, 1985. Terms and prices subject to change. Your enrollment is subject to acceptance by Simon & Schuster Enterprises.

Silhouette Special Edition

MORE ROMANCE FOR
A SPECIAL WAY TO RELAX

$1.95 each

2 ☐ Hastings	21 ☐ Hastings	41 ☐ Halston	60 ☐ Thorne
3 ☐ Dixon	22 ☐ Howard	42 ☐ Drummond	61 ☐ Beckman
4 ☐ Vitek	23 ☐ Charles	43 ☐ Shaw	62 ☐ Bright
5 ☐ Converse	24 ☐ Dixon	44 ☐ Eden	63 ☐ Wallace
6 ☐ Douglass	25 ☐ Hardy	45 ☐ Charles	64 ☐ Converse
7 ☐ Stanford	26 ☐ Scott	46 ☐ Howard	65 ☐ Cates
8 ☐ Halston	27 ☐ Wisdom	47 ☐ Stephens	66 ☐ Mikels
9 ☐ Baxter	28 ☐ Ripy	48 ☐ Ferrell	67 ☐ Shaw
10 ☐ Thiels	29 ☐ Bergen	49 ☐ Hastings	68 ☐ Sinclair
11 ☐ Thornton	30 ☐ Stephens	50 ☐ Browning	69 ☐ Dalton
12 ☐ Sinclair	31 ☐ Baxter	51 ☐ Trent	70 ☐ Clare
13 ☐ Beckman	32 ☐ Douglass	52 ☐ Sinclair	71 ☐ Skillern
14 ☐ Keene	33 ☐ Palmer	53 ☐ Thomas	72 ☐ Belmont
15 ☐ James	35 ☐ James	54 ☐ Hohl	73 ☐ Taylor
16 ☐ Carr	36 ☐ Dailey	55 ☐ Stanford	74 ☐ Wisdom
17 ☐ John	37 ☐ Stanford	56 ☐ Wallace	75 ☐ John
18 ☐ Hamilton	38 ☐ John	57 ☐ Thornton	76 ☐ Ripy
19 ☐ Shaw	39 ☐ Milan	58 ☐ Douglass	77 ☐ Bergen
20 ☐ Musgrave	40 ☐ Converse	59 ☐ Roberts	78 ☐ Gladstone

$2.25 each

79 ☐ Hastings	87 ☐ Dixon	95 ☐ Doyle	103 ☐ Taylor
80 ☐ Douglass	88 ☐ Saxon	96 ☐ Baxter	104 ☐ Wallace
81 ☐ Thornton	89 ☐ Meriwether	97 ☐ Shaw	105 ☐ Sinclair
82 ☐ McKenna	90 ☐ Justin	98 ☐ Hurley	106 ☐ John
83 ☐ Major	91 ☐ Stanford	99 ☐ Dixon	107 ☐ Ross
84 ☐ Stephens	92 ☐ Hamilton	100 ☐ Roberts	108 ☐ Stephens
85 ☐ Beckman	93 ☐ Lacey	101 ☐ Bergen	109 ☐ Beckman
86 ☐ Halston	94 ☐ Barrie	102 ☐ Wallace	110 ☐ Browning

Silhouette Special Edition

$2.25 each

111 ☐ Thorne	133 ☐ Douglass	155 ☐ Lacey	177 ☐ Howard
112 ☐ Belmont	134 ☐ Ripy	156 ☐ Hastings	178 ☐ Bishop
113 ☐ Camp	135 ☐ Seger	157 ☐ Taylor	179 ☐ Meriwether
114 ☐ Ripy	136 ☐ Scott	158 ☐ Charles	180 ☐ Jackson
115 ☐ Halston	137 ☐ Parker	159 ☐ Camp	181 ☐ Browning
116 ☐ Roberts	138 ☐ Thornton	160 ☐ Wisdom	182 ☐ Thornton
117 ☐ Converse	139 ☐ Halston	161 ☐ Stanford	183 ☐ Sinclair
118 ☐ Jackson	140 ☐ Sinclair	162 ☐ Roberts	184 ☐ Daniels
119 ☐ Langan	141 ☐ Saxon	163 ☐ Halston	185 ☐ Gordon
120 ☐ Dixon	142 ☐ Bergen	164 ☐ Ripy	186 ☐ Scott
121 ☐ Shaw	143 ☐ Bright	165 ☐ Lee	187 ☐ Stanford
122 ☐ Walker	144 ☐ Meriwether	166 ☐ John	188 ☐ Lacey
123 ☐ Douglass	145 ☐ Wallace	167 ☐ Hurley	189 ☐ Ripy
124 ☐ Mikels	146 ☐ Thornton	168 ☐ Thornton	190 ☐ Wisdom
125 ☐ Cates	147 ☐ Dalton	169 ☐ Beckman	191 ☐ Hardy
126 ☐ Wildman	148 ☐ Gordon	170 ☐ Paige	192 ☐ Taylor
127 ☐ Taylor	149 ☐ Claire	171 ☐ Gray	
128 ☐ Macomber	150 ☐ Dailey	172 ☐ Hamilton	
129 ☐ Rowe	151 ☐ Shaw	173 ☐ Belmont	
130 ☐ Carr	152 ☐ Adams	174 ☐ Dixon	
131 ☐ Lee	153 ☐ Sinclair	175 ☐ Roberts	
132 ☐ Dailey	154 ☐ Malek	176 ☐ Walker	

SILHOUETTE SPECIAL EDITION, Department SE/2
1230 Avenue of the Americas
New York, NY 10020

Please send me the books I have checked above. I am enclosing $_____ (please add 75¢ to cover postage and handling). NYS and NYC residents please add appropriate sales tax). Send check or money order—no cash or C.O.D.'s please. Allow six weeks for delivery.

NAME _____

ADDRESS _____

CITY _____ STATE/ZIP _____